There was a Mr. Cristi

There was a Mr. Cristi

Raymond Knister

Black Moss Press
Windsor, Ontario
2006

© Imogen Knister Givens, 2006

National Library and Archives Canada Cataloguing in Publication

Knister, Raymond, 1899-1932.
    There was a Mr. Cristi / Raymond Knister.

ISBN 0-88753-414-7

    I. Title.

PS8521.N75T43 2006   C813'.52   C2006-900642-3

Cover Image: p7575 from Windsor Community Museum

Published by Black Moss Press at 2450 Byng Road, Windsor, Ontario N8W3E8.

Black Moss Press acknowledges the generous support of The Canada Council for the Arts and the Ontario Arts Council for its publishing program.

Le Conseil des Arts du Canada | The Canada Council for the Arts

ONTARIO ARTS COUNCIL
CONSEIL DES ARTS DE L'ONTARIO

Table of Contents

Acknowledgements
General Preface
A Note on the Text

There Was A Mr. Cristi	*11*
The Inheritance Of The Meek	*14*
She Should Be Older	*17*
Potatoes À La Cristi	*24*
Mr. Bedlington And Belle	*33*
Mrs. Webster	*41*
On A Due-Due-Dewey Day	*48*
Curling Irons And Irony	*52*
Moving In	*57*
Baby Visits Daddy	*61*
Mrs. Webster Mends	*65*
Le Médecin Malgré Lui	*69*
Fur Coat	*73*
Mr. Bedlington Pays A Call	*77*
The Taste In Her Mouth	*81*
Bathroom Confidences	*89*
Green Eyed Monster	*92*
Christmas Negotiations	*96*
Christmas Holidays	*100*
No Anchor But Anger	*104*
Lidas Father	*111*
Climax For Creditors	*116*
So Dark! Or The Hindu From The Window	*120*
Vaccinations	*124*
Points of Vantage	*127*
England, My England	*132*
Mr. Cristi Comes Into His Own	*136*

for Minnie Gamble Acton-Bond

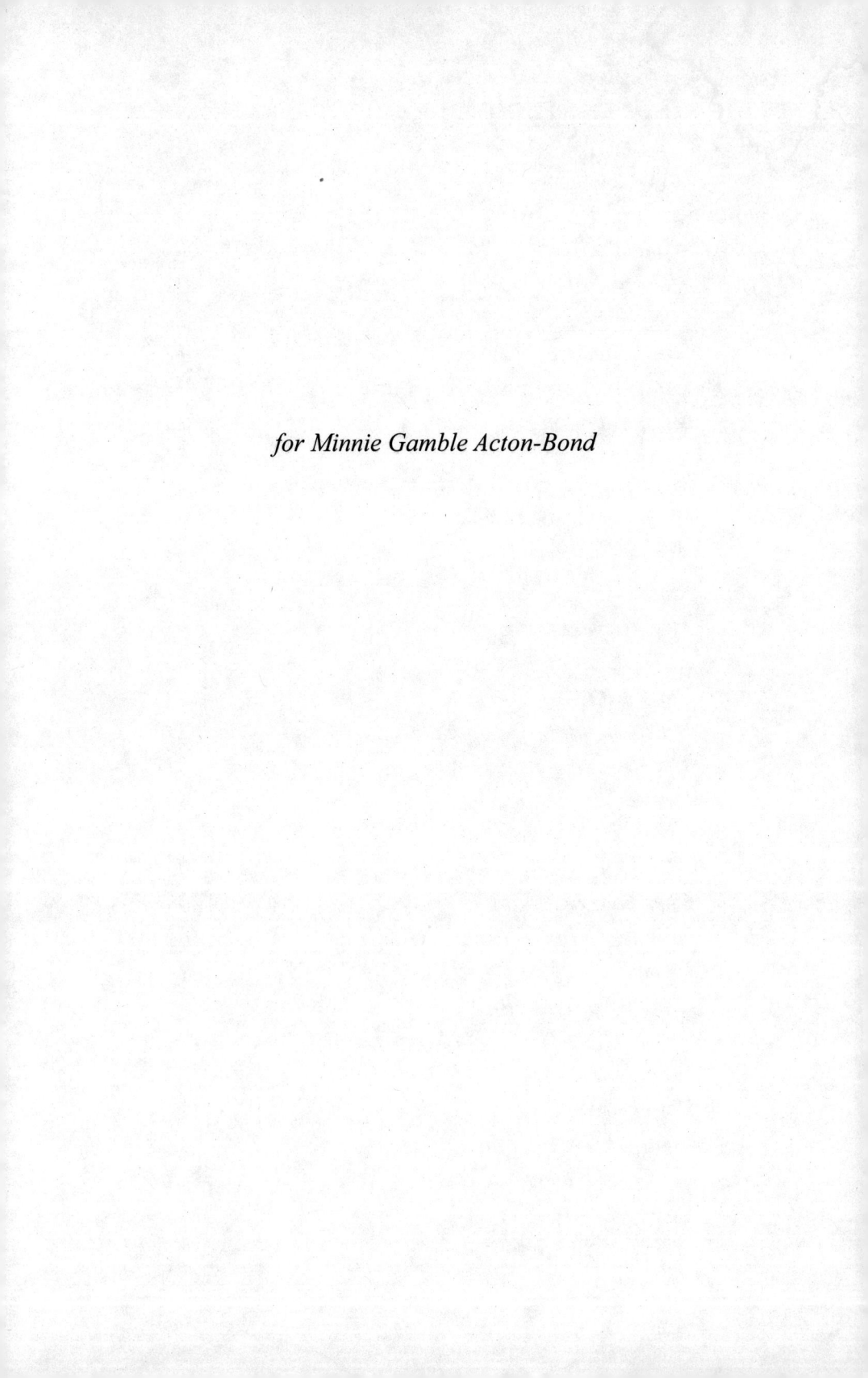

Acknowledgements

A special word of thanks is due to Imogen Knister Givens for her tireless commitment to her father's legacy in Canadian literature. Also thank you to Marty Gervais and Stephen Pender for their guidance and expertise.

Publication acknowledgements are due to the following people for their work on the design layout and editing of this novel: Lindsey Bannister, Maryszka Clovis, Jamie Gaunt, Laurie Gibson, Stefanie Helbich, Caitlin McNamara, James Prophet, Marissa Reaume, Lindsey Rivait, Melanie Santarossa, Devon Stinchcombe, Sonia Sulaiman, Brendan Thomas, Meighan Topolnicki, Ryan Turgeon, Lindsay Turner, Ben Van Dongen, and Michael John Wheeler.

General Preface

A pioneer Canadian modernist, Raymond Knister and his work have been celebrated for seventy-five years. His innovative writing lucidly captures the simplicity, as well as the duplicity, of everyday life. As Knister wrote in 1928, "Many thousands of Canadians are learning to see their own daily lives, and to demand its presentment with realism." Besides a large collection of poetry, short stories and critical essays and the popular novels *White Narcissus* (1929) and *My Star Predominant* (1934), *There Was a Mr. Cristi*, available here for the first time, is a novel of frustrated aspirations, petty deception, and stinging humanity; Knister's complex characters illustrate how the 'human' is an unfinished project.

The novel, according to Knister's daughter, Imogen Knister Givens, was inspired by Knister's sister-in-law Minnie Gamble and her experiences in a Toronto rooming house. Many of the novel's characters and situations are drawn from actual individuals who his sister-in-law encountered during her stay. Amusingly, the integral Ms. Campbell character was inspired by Minnie herself.

After Knister's death in 1932, his wife gave her sister, Minnie, the original manuscript in memory of Raymond, as many of the stories he intertwined in the novel were the same stories she had once shared with him regarding her time spent in a Toronto rooming house during the 1920s. Ultimately, it seems Knister's world renowned authorship was shadowed by the Great Depression and Second World War yet with new interest in Canadian heritage since the 1970's his work is once again being celebrated and recognized. Although this novel was never forgotten, Minnie Gamble Acton-Bond retained the only copy. However in the 1990's, Imogen Givens, the author's daughter, asked Mary Harris, Minnie's daughter, to try and locate it, and once the manuscript was found it was returned to Imogen Givens.

"I think it is great that there is an interest in my father and his work. For me, the characters seem to come to life when I read it." Givens recognizes qualities of her mother, family and friends in Knister's characters. "I can picture my Aunt Minnie in the story." Miss Campbell in the story is recognizably Minnie Gamble. Raymond Knister also gives himself and his wife Myrtle a cameo appearance as Mr. And Mrs. Max Helyar. The description of Miss Campbell's sister as, "another dark girl, taller and heavier, healthy looking" is of Myrtle Knister, and her husband is described as, "a ruddy-faced, stocky, slender fellow, with a way of looking at you as though he might want to laugh." Knister's Chicago Taxi-Driver's licence confirms that description, especially the picture on it. This "Max Helyar" outwits the over-bearing landlady and a by-stander says, "She met her match." Knister wrote a non-fiction story about his fight with a Montreal landlord in "A Brush With Quebec Law", printed in *Raymond Knister, Poems, Stories and Essays*.

For the first time, Black Moss Press is proud to publish *There Was a Mr. Cristi*, a story that allows readers a glimpse into the private lives of an assortment of people living in a Toronto rooming-house during the 1920s. The novel centers on a powerful self-revelation by Mrs. Cristi: one's true identity can never be altered.

A Note on the Text

This text was discovered as an unedited manuscript that remained unpublished during the author's lifetime. As an editorial team we have regularized the spelling of names, corrected spelling and grammatical errors, and otherwise made minor changes which would have been made had Raymond Knister participated in the production and publication of the text. Our central concern was to stay true to the original manuscript and to produce a text that is readable to a modern audience without jeopardising its historical merit or the voice of the author.

There Was A Mr. Cristi

You would guess that he was Italian, but the name was pronounced Christie so casually you understood that he might be English, if you had never seen him, only his wife. He was tall, dark, and good-looking in a placid way, she would imply. He had a fruit farm outside of Toronto, and in general bore himself as a transplanted person of means and, perhaps, family. As a young man he visited England, where he married an Englishwoman, tall and fair, with quick speech and mannerisms. They had three children, Belle, Carlotta, and Edmund. Belle was born in England, and they took her with them when they went to Switzerland for the better part of a year. Then Mrs. Cristi formed a penchant for Canada, as she pictured it. She felt sure of a fitting place in the society of the colony. Mr. Cristi had given in, sooner or later, to all her expressed desires, and he came to Canada. Carlotta and Edmund were born in Toronto. Even in this country their marital relations were not happy. Mrs. Cristi was not satisfied, though he swore that he did not know what she wanted. She did not like farm life, for one thing. After she had left him, she would say, "And he had no waterworks in the house, if you can imagine that." He would not make any special attempts upon Society, but was content with acquaintances, friendships formed through chance. She had the car some afternoons, but instead of associating with the Port Credit set, she drove to Toronto, shopped and window-shopped, and at four-thirty had tea in the Arcadian Court. Excited by the orchestra and the well-dressed women about her, she assured herself that if she could live in Toronto she would soon be mingling with the best people. But she would need a different husband for that, she thought with a wry face. Their quarrels became worse. He would not give her as much as she demanded to spend, and finally, she had him summoned to court, charged with non-support. Rather than submit he appeared and defended himself. The court did not give her judgement so she told her husband that since he would not support her she would go to Toronto and support the children herself. Belle, now seventeen, had sided with her mother, and was eager to go.

Mrs. Cristi had friends in Toronto, Mr. and Mrs. Kennedy, who kept a rooming house. After staying with them two weeks, enjoying the city, she thought it criminal to waste the experience she gained. She knew exactly how such a business should be run. She went first to the real estate agency which rented apartments and houses, and was given a salesman and a car. As she rode about town she explained to the man that she had to have something unusual, refined-looking, something distinguished. If her people in England could see her now! But the man stopped the car at some terrible houses. Lots of them she wouldn't even sniff at. She'd tell him to drive on.

"I want a house with vines creeping down over the windows. You know what I mean; they look as though the whole house was overgrown with vines, just overgrown."

"Like they'd grew up the other side and come down over the roof on this side, eh?" asked the agent good-naturedly. She was an entertaining woman to drive with, and smart-looking, but somewhat more notional than most.

Then they found the house she wanted. It was on an old residential side-street, less than a block from the car-line and a district of shopping and apartment hotels. As soon as Mrs. Cristi saw this tall old house—three stories, dark brick with great bow-window, and overgrown with vines—she cried out:

"I'll take this one no matter what it costs."

She was out of the car in an instant, and running—the tall stiff woman actually running about from one room to another, up stairs and down. The whole house was lovely. Great large rooms in front on the first and second floors, with fireplaces. Ordinary bedrooms at the back and on the third floor. Two bathrooms, on the second and third floors. And it was practically all furnished. It just needed something of her very own choosing. She could rent a few pieces that would give the place an air. She thoughtfully pulled her pearl earring forward on her ear. Splendid! She wouldn't feel cramped and out of place here with her kiddies, she said. Everything was lovely. "What's the price?" The agency man named top price. Before he brought up his reinforcements of sales talk, she dropped: "I'll take it," and was rattling on about rearranging furniture. She was a well-satisfied prospective tenant. Such a house was not rented every day, and the agent thought it could be arranged that she pay rent for the first month at its termination, instead of in advance, if she would give a note for the amount.

That night she talked to the Kennedys and Belle and Carlotta. After her children were put to bed, she got her friends to agree to back her note. There was no risk to them, because if she could not make the house pay at once they could come over and show her her mistakes. Besides, she had money coming from her husband, whom she had sued. It was all clear. The following afternoon they moved her luggage into the house.

The Inheritance Of The Meek

Mr. Bedlington, the landlord, was a nice man. He was a little bachelor with mild manners who felt that everyone did the best he could. He was forced to see when they had been in his house over a month, that the Cristis had no aptitude for running a rooming house. In fact, Mrs. Cristi told him that they could not make it pay, and begged him not to call on Mr. Kennedy for the money. Neither of them could have said how it came to be proposed that Mr. Bedlington come to live with them in the house, supervise it, and see that it paid its way.

Taking his meals with them, he silently objected to the expensive food and wasteful buying, but he would not have cared to interfere, even if Mrs. Cristi's manner had permitted such a thought. He wanted to help them and himself, and to do that he had to make the best of their ways. He kept busy. There were a lot of little changes to be made in the way of improvements, little things to be bought. In the evenings, he worked at a closed-in back porch he was building on the second floor, when he did not have to balance his ledgers, which included accounts of labour and materials for two new duplex houses he was building out on Yonge Street North.

Mr. Bedlington was a contractor by profession. He had been born a country boy, the youngest of a shiftless family which he left in order to labour at a barn building. Later, he became a carpenter, saved all the money he could, bought a house in Toronto, rented it, and went on working. Then he undertook to build a two-flat house himself. He remained as saving as when he first left home, wore cheap clothes, drove a small car which he laid up in the winter, and never married. He was about forty years old, small, and straight, and genteel looking no matter what he was doing. He went about the house quietly and meekly, and felt that the Cristis did not like him to be in the parlour. Roomers met him in the hall in shirt sleeves, carrying a saw or hammer, and boards he had sawn in the cellar. He would pause at a distance to make way for them, with a timid hopeful smile for greeting. Eyes swimming behind thick glasses. Brown face. Hair fair and crisply frizzy, baldness appearing beyond the shiny round forehead. They did not know who he was unless they had been told.

The rooms were not all occupied now. Downstairs, besides the great Cristi front parlour there was another large room divided into a dinning-room, sleeping-sleeve, and kitchenette, where Mrs. Wilson lived. Her two sons, law students, had a room on the third floor, but they ate their meals here. The Cristis kitchen, also large, completed the first floor.

On the second floor the front room with the marble fireplace was vacant. Then there was the Cristis bedroom, then the stairs down and up; and off the lower hall another large room was occupied by two girls. It had a fireplace and a gas stove. Then came separate toilet and bath, and a small room at the back, where Mr. Bedlington slept, and off it the back porch he was building.

On the third floor there was a small front room with a balcony, then the room the law students had, next the larger middle room used by a business girl, Lida O'Ryan, the bath, and at the back a little room usually vacant but just now inhabited by a young fellow working in a garage, whom they called Bill.

Sometimes Mr. Bedlington wondered whether there was any

way of making this house pay. The Cristis did not seem to be cut out for rooming house keepers. They did not seem to attract the right kind of people. At best, a careless, easy-going type of roomer, and at worst, downright sporty-looking gentlemen whom Mrs. Cristi introduced to him as dear friends of hers and who made jokes he could not understand. There was one fellow, a Sam Bernie, who, Mr. Bedlington thought, must make his living playing the races and who seemed likely to establish himself as Mrs. Cristi's steady company. It didn't look right, but what could you say to a woman like her? Then, she had all kinds of assurance and would not listen to even his advice about running the house, if she had not been constrained thereto. He gave her what she demanded, replying to her urgings in a quiet, pleasant tone. There had to be give and take on both sides. Tenants and landlords could not get along without one another. Nevertheless, he had misgivings, and he asked himself how all this was going to turn out.

She Should Be Older

One afternoon in December, a slight dark young lady in a black coat and a white fur cap came to the house and wanted to look at a room. She had been out of town, but formerly she had lived in this district and she liked it. She had taken a position as governess a few blocks away, across the ravine in Rosedale.

She was met at the door by Mrs. Cristi in person. Mrs. Cristi was dressed in a blue dress, very short—she and Belle shared it—cut in a low V and shaped at the waist. She was wearing a small-brimmed black hat, well on one side, with her hair up over one ear—an earring showing—and down over the other side. She was tall and stately, melodramatically abrupt in a staged English manner.

"Surely I'll show you the room." She whirled away, and trudged, with a deliberation contrasted with her speech, up the stairs to a large room at the side of the house. The girl saw that it faced a big-windowed school across the yard, and it had a fireplace with a gilt mirror, windows at either side with very dirty curtains. There was a day-bed, a round dining table with chairs to match, a china cabinet, and a stove. The place had not recently been cleaned. The stove and even the floor were greasy.

"I just felt so discouraged when those girls left I haven't had a thing done to this room. They really were the nastiest pair of girls

I ever saw. They said they'd be here indefinitely—they were here when I took the house over—and they left within a month. I don't care. I'm just glad they're gone. They were the nastiest girls I ever saw. Just ask Belle."

The girl had been listening absently. Evidently she had rented rooms before.

"I would have to have the room right away if I took it. I'd move in tomorrow. But I would like to have a bureau with a glass instead of the china cabinet. And of course you won't leave any pipes about the wall when the stove is taken out. I like this room, but it is a little large, and I dare say expensive."

"Don't you worry about that, my dear," said Mrs. Cristi, fidgeting and touching her arm. "Don't you ever worry. We'll fix you up, make you comfortable. I know how it is myself. You want something that just suits your taste or else you'd rather not be rooming. You'll know just what you want the minute you see it. Now won't you? I know just what you're like. You like this room, don't you! But maybe you'd prefer to see another room before you decide. Come on, my dear, we have another room upstairs."

They went upstairs to the third floor and entered another large room just above the one at which they had been looking. It had no fireplace, and the two side windows were small. But it had a book-case, two couches—one wide and one narrow—a table and several rocking chairs. The girl fancied a rose parlour lamp beside one couch.

"A nice place to read," she said.

"I rather promised this room to Bill," Mrs. Cristi explained, twitching her hat to another angle, raising the blind of one of the windows, and adjusting her dress at the hips.

"Bill has the little room at the back, and he wanted to get this room as soon as it was vacant, you see the girl who has it now will be moving out in the morning. But Bill wouldn't greatly care if I explained to him that *you* preferred it."

It seemed to the young lady that she was fortunate, but though she was very much present and Bill was absent, she declined to take advantage of this fact.

"I really like the other room better," she said. "Perhaps I'd better look at that one again." She implied that possibly a discrepancy in their views of price might be adjusted.

They entered the hall and began to descend the stairs, and the hush which had embraced the house was suddenly rent by a howl from the room next the one they had been examining. Though it seemed an involuntary half-laughing screech, the girl looked around nervously. Mrs. Cristi chattered gaily and jolted briskly down the stairs.

Back in the big room a bargain was struck. The iron was hot for stipulations: those curtains were really appalling.

"You'll see that the room is arranged for me, will you? The curtains..."

"Of course, of course! Those girls! The curtains were perfectly clean when they came and now look at them. Come in here, and we'll talk it over."

They went into the front room with the white marble fireplace. The girl felt affection for these old rooms already. And Mrs. Cristi was unusual too. They sat down and began to talk, Mrs. Cristi's air and hat supplying invisible tea. The girl now saw that she was quite cleverly made up, and the colour went well with the fair hair showing beneath the hat. But she must be older; the hair itself was streaked with grey when you examined it.

Mrs. Cristi had been taking notice of her visitor's white fur hat.

"Where did you get such a lovely *hat*! So different, and it becomes you so well, with your dark hair."

"I had it made specially, because I have been spending part of the winter in Northern Ontario. It does look unusual here."

"I wonder how I'd look in one like that. How did you like Northern Ontario?" Mrs. Cristi's impulsive words seemed to swirl about the girl like a cascade about a rock. Manifestly it was only the formality of the girl's bearing which precluded endless query and exclamations.

"Why, it's interesting of course. But there were so few girls there of my own age, you know. The proportion of men, unmarried men, and girls must be ten to one. So of course one doesn't have many girlfriends. That makes it rather lonesome."

"Oh, I'd just love to go up there. I think it would be a lovely place, and I've read about the North Country, you know? It would be wonderful. The men are so big up there, aren't they? Wonderful country. I'd love to go."

"Even when there are so few girls?"

"Yes, that would just suit me, even though there were no women at all. I distrust girls!"

The house had been quiet again, the door of the room was half open, and now they heard a heavy bouncing tread down the hall. A great round yellow head appeared around the door, at a surprising height.

"Come in Belle. This is Belle," said Mrs. Cristi. "My daughter, Miss Campbell."

A mountainous rounded fair girl, with thick, glowing honey-coloured features, bounced into the room and across it. She wore a black crepe-back satin skirt which reached from her knees half-way to the waist, topped by a white cotton camisole, sleeveless and without a jacket.

"Glad to meet you, I'm sure, Miss. Campbell," Belle said in a ringing voice, with the most cordial of smiles. She plumped down into an arm chair.

Her mother went on talking nicely. The little dark slight girl gazed occasionally at Belle with awe—she was bulging with fat and muscle and apparent animal spirits. She seemed to be about twenty.

"I'm sending my second daughter, Carlotta, to convent. The

Sisters are so wonderful. I love them, Miss Campbell...love them. Such lovely characters. It's such a wonderful thing for a child's manners. Don't you think so, Miss—of course one doesn't have to be told such things. You know yourself."

"You go to the Catholic church, then?" asked the girl in surprise.

"No, I'm a High Anglican myself, but I think the Sisters are so wonderful. I declare, here come the boys."

There were heavy staggering steps in the hall, scrapping sounds on the walls, and an occasional shout. Then a stocky young man entered the room, bearing a six-year-old boy on his shoulders, a round-faced, brown-haired, Buster-Brown sort of youngster.

"I didn't want him to bring me in here," said the boy avoiding their eyes.

"This is Bill," Mrs. Cristi introduced the young man. "You know Bill's a southerner. He comes from the South."

"The sunny south," corrected Bill with a grin. His voice indicated removed adenoids. He was a blue-eyed fair fellow, and spoke with a slight Irish brogue. He balanced the child on his shoulders, and seized him below the calves.

"Stand up!" he commanded. "That's the way the Cossack soldiers do it, they stand right up on top of their horses at full gallop. Stand up. I'm holding you."

The boy shakily stiffened his legs, and standing erect in Bill's grip he seized the chandelier by its brass piping.

"Now I'm going to let you go," announced Bill.

Edmund, the boy, grappled with the chandelier, then seized one bracket as Bill removed his hands from his legs. Then the mantle and electric bulb and Edmund descended toward the floor, rapidly, noisily, but safely. A wiring cord hung down from the chandelier. Edmund let go. The wire and fixture dangled in mid-air.

Mrs. Cristi noticed this incident in the midst of her conversation.

"Now you have done it," she remarked.

"Bill made me do it," said the boy.

"Such poor curtains as they left us in the house," said Mrs. Cristi to her caller. "Just look at those!"

The big windows were expensively, even luxuriously, curtained. Miss Campbell said nothing, wondering momentarily whether Mrs. Cristi would rent the room just as it stood, with its broken chandelier.

Bill got Edmund on his shoulders again; then, he reached around with his other hand for the bulb, which he gave the boy. He raised it toward the ceiling, and told Edmund to shove it back into place. Edmund wrestled with the bulb and the chandelier in mid-air and tried to adjust them. Belle spoke up.

"Bill, what do you want to be fooling around that way for? It'll cost three or four dollars to fix that. You ought to know better. You're always rough housing with that kid." Her mouth said without expression. She turned and listened to her mother's conversation.

"Oh, we'll fix it," said Bill cheerfully. "Just watch us."

"Go on out. I'll fix it," said Belle commandingly.

She sat back in the deep chair however, and Edmund took up the fixture and examined it. After some study, he lifted and tried to hold it and at the same time shove the wiring into the aperture. The women went on talking.

"Miss Campbell," said Mrs. Cristi, "we'll wash those curtains in your room right away, and iron them. Belle you go out and see to that right away, will you?"

"Yes, mamma."

"Yes, I think I'll enjoy that room with the fireplace, Mrs. Cristi," said Miss Campbell. She has a taste for the people as well as for the house. They seemed interesting and unconstrained.

"We'll see to it right away. Don't you worry, Miss Campbell. We know you want things nice. You just tell us about anything you want, and we'll get it for you. Or if I'm not here—I go out on occasion—Belle will take care of you."

"Oh, I'm sure I'll like it," said Miss Campbell.

After thy had talked a few minutes longer in a social-business manner of getting acquainted, she went away, saying that she would move in the following day, but that she might be back that evening. By this time Edmund had succeeded in getting the bulb back among its fellows in the chandelier. It was late afternoon.

Potatoes à La Cristi

So much more every week, Mrs. Cristi had Miss Campbell's money in her pocket. The rooms were getting pretty well filled now, and she beamed upon Belle and Carlotta as she descended into the kitchen. Carlotta, fourteen years old, glowered back in return. A good deal of time she was wishing they lived with her father, and when she missed him she was not in a very good humour with her mother. She was dark, unlike the other two children, and more neatly built, prettier than Belle.

"Well, dears," said Mrs. Cristi. "What shall we have for supper? We should have something especially nice. Maybe Miss Campbell will be back in time to have it with us. Wouldn't it be nice to make her at home the first night she's here?"

"Fancy she won't," said Carlotta, who had peeped through the hall to watch the new roomer depart.

"Would chicken croquettes be nice? What do you think?"

"We haven't any chicken."

"We could buy croquettes already made, at the delicatessen," suggested Belle.

"Oh girls, don't bother going out for anything, girls. It's so cold. We've got lots of potatoes, and I'll make a dish of scalloped potatoes. Won't that be nice? You know you like them, Baby."

"No milk," Carlotta replied without bothering to look in the cupboard.

"Well, go out and get some milk then," said Belle, robustly.

While the girls were quarrelling about this, Mrs. Cristi dashed down the cellar stairs and came up with a large bag partly filled with potatoes, and her hat still on her head. She energetically put water over the gas burner, and began to peel potatoes.

"Baby, come get me salt and pepper for these, so it'll be ready. Edmund, get some water to wash the potatoes in when I have them peeled." The boy had come into the room with a penitent expression, feeling that it was time a meal should be made.

Belle wondered whether there were any onions in the house.

"Yes, we do need an onion to give a flavour. When you get the milk at the store, get some onions. Edmund, you're the boy to go to the store, aren't you!"

"What store will I get the milk at?" asked Edmund, interested now. He liked to take a list with him to the store, and hold the paper folded in his hand while he recited his mother's requirements to the clerk. He would hand over the list, then some other boy, bigger than himself, would take the groceries to his home. Once they left the store at the same time and went along together; but the other boy wouldn't talk.

"McCready's, of course," said his mother briefly. "And tell them to give the milk to you. You bring it. Remember Edmund."

"Why can't I go to the red store where the lady had sample soup that day?"

"You do what you're told and go on." She smiled at Edmund, though. He swung a foot and watched her peeling the potatoes, then turned and picked his cap up from a chair. Baby went with him to the front door, repeating directions.

"We must be getting a pretty bill there, Mother," said Belle.

"Oh, Belle!" screamed her mother, "Run to the 'phone and call McCready's and tell them to give Edmund some onions."

Belle bounded away, but down the hall she heard her mother again:

"Oh wait, we have a bag of onions in the cellar."

She enjoyed these occasional flurries of activity and even thought they should come more frequently, she knew dimly that what her mother required was a suggestor, someone to suggest things to do. But, though Belle knew when the windows needed washing and the floor scrubbing, she was so little inclined to such exercises herself that she did not blame anyone who neglected them. But she was sure that her mother needed her to stand by now that they did not have her father. She was glad of freedom, but it has responsibilities.

By and by, in a chaos of potato peelings, muddy water, tins and dishes, milk-bottles, onion-skins, and a weeping Belle peeling the onions, a casserole full of sliced raw potatoes was accumulated, bread crumbs sprinkled over the top, and three great chunks of bread added.

"Oh, we need cheese. Now you will have to call McCready's before Edmund gets away. Baby, why don't you turn on the oven burner?"

Belle got to the 'phone just as Mrs. Wells was coming out of her room to call her sons on the third floor to supper. Belle grinned at her and sat down to the 'phone.

"McCready's!" said Mrs. Wells. "Surely you don't deal at McCready's. They're the dearest place in the city. They simply hold you up, that's what they do. I wouldn't deal there for anything."

Mrs. Wells disappeared; her boys were clattering down the two flights of stairs to supper.

In time the Cristi meal was served. It consisted of the great bowl of scalloped potatoes, roasted to the rich orange of fried cheese, and tea. There was also bread and a pat of butter and a new bottle of olives, an after-thought of Edmund's. It was seven o'clock and everyone felt listless and hollow.

"Aren't we going to have tarts or nothing?"

Edmund appeared in the kitchen to survey the prospects when it had occurred to him that he was too hungry to wait any longer. He had been whiling the time after his return from the grocery in Bill's room.

"Why didn't I bring tarts?"

There had been a run on tarts in the family—those swell buttered black currant ones the delicatessen lady made.

"Why, we're having scalloped potatoes, Edmund boy!" exclaimed his mother.

"Yes, but I want tarts or pudding or something too."

"The girls didn't want anything else," he was informed.

"Aw—I bet Bill's hungry, anyhow."

"Go and tell him to come to supper."

Bill had been accustomed to taking his meals with the Cristis since he had been laid off work. When he came to them, a couple of weeks ago, he had been working three days a week, in a garage, and that was why his hands were always dirty. Now he was off altogether for a few weeks, but he was so much one of the family he didn't mind it; time did not hang heavy.

Mrs. Cristi knew that Bill would appreciate her cooking. He was a good-natured healthy young fellow, and had taken a great fancy to Belle when she showed him the rooms. Mrs. Cristi always felt gayer when he was about, and encouraged their friendship. She felt younger than Belle. Belle worried sometimes.

Edmund listened to Bill's praises, but liked him without knowing why.

"Say this is swell," said Bill, when he appeared with his slouchy hipped walk. His hair was shining; he was wearing an old sweater and his shirt open at the neck. "Mrs. Cristi, you sure know how to encourage the inner man."

"Belle will be here in a minute," said Mrs. Cristi. "She's gone down to the cellar to hunt some fruit. Mr. Bedlington told us there were a few cans of fruit he brought with him from his other house, and we could use them if we cared to."

"Sure. Sporting old guy, ain't he?" said Bill. He looked upon the mild forty-year-old Mr. Bedlington with the tolerance of the owner of the goose that laid the golden egg.

"Mr. Bedlington is what I call a real gentleman," said Mrs. Cristi. "He's just right." She spoke in the tone of one soothing a child, or petting a kitten. "Too bad he has to wear glasses."

"Yeah, you're right at that," agreed Bill. "Say, you got the chairs up yourself Edmund, eh?"

"You bet I did." Edmund clicked his tongue against his teeth.

"Mother, where's Lida?" Belle asked, with two dusty quart jars on her forearm.

"Taking her bath. Getting ready to go out tonight."

"Does anyone know where Lida is?" No one heard anyone else talking.

Lida was now the Cristi's maid. She lost her office job and Mrs. Cristi let her do housework for her room and board. She was small and dark and solidly well-formed; she seldom wore stocking unless she was going out. Her hair was about two inches long about her head, and very wiry and chewed-looking from curling and burning. In daytime she wore a red ribbon around her forehead while she went about her work, and the hair on top of her head looked particularly stringy and patchy, like that of a long-haired calf which had been lying in damp places in wintertime.

Lida knew some classy fellows, however, from her office days, and she introduced Mrs. Cristi to new ones from time to time. Some evenings the two of them went out alone, and returned later with new men. Mrs. Cristi thought a good deal of Lida, and depended upon her for good times of what would otherwise be dull evenings. She advised Lida to hunt for a job, but did not worry when Lida said she had to get stockings, or overslept till it was too late to apply.

Lately the train of Lida's suitors had been narrowing down. There was a young dentist who was pursuing her wildly, and Lida was quite as wildly in love with him. She thought he was a kind of mystery man, for she did not know where he lived, and he was never in when she called him by the 'phone. Some kid by the name of Zimmie took her messages, and Dr. Heslan got them alright. At least he said he was Dr. Heslan, a dentist, but judging from things he dropped, Lida thought he might be a millionaire's son incognito. So it came about that Mrs. Cristi was neglected in their jaunts, and they went alone. It was rather hard sometimes to get a fellow for her anyway. Other nights they stayed in, and left the lights out.

"Goin' with the doctor fellow?" asked Bill indifferently.

"Sh– Sh–" said Mrs. Cristi. "She might be coming."

There was a shrill tra-la-la of song on the stairs, and Lida came down the narrow hallway to the kitchen, dressed in pale green chiffon, with a bunch of flowers at the shoulder.

"Come on Lida! 'At a girl," called Bill. "Nourishment is in sight now. You're on the home stretch." He was tired of waiting.

"Yeh, I'm coming, Bill," returned Lida from the hall.

They all sat down. Mrs. Cristi paid no attention to the new arrival nor did she remark upon having prepared the meal herself with no assistance save that of her family. She had forgotten all about Lida, in her creative zest. Now she sighed contentedly, sat down, and removed her hat, which she tossed upon a kitchen cabinet. Nobody served. The maid tidied and swept the halls, but at mealtime she forgot that she was the maid. Everyone was in a mood receptive to whatever might come his way. There was a taste to even the bread and butter.

Before the meal had well begun the telephone rang in the hall, and Mrs. Cristi rose and strode out.

"Hello, hellaou, halleaou!"

A voice said something while she was helloing, and now it began to repeat.

"Yes, this is Mrs. Cristi, herself speaking. What is it you want to speak to me about?"

The person at the other end of the line waited until there was a pause in the crepitating yells, like those of *Craig's Wife*, but before she could hang up the receiver on him in the manner of that lady, he announced:

"This is Mr. McCready speaking. Your charge account for groceries at our store has become a substantial one, Mrs. Cristi. Payment is due at the end of each month, and you have not paid anything for going on two months. We would appreciate it if you would settle with us tomorrow, Mrs. Cristi." The even heavy flowing voice bore her down.

"Why, what do you mean? What do you mean by saying that you give credit when you don't?"

"Credit up to certain limits, Mrs. Cristi. But when those limits are past there is no more credit."

"I shall have my patronage removed to another shop at once. I certainly shall. It's preposterous. I shall!" she exclaimed breathlessly. Her toe tapped upon the hall floor. She had settled him. She'd hang up.

"Well, in any case, better settle up with us before you send any more orders. When that is done we shall be quite prepared to give you credit again. I shall be making some collections in your district tonight. Will you be home about nine o'clock?"

"Nonsense! You are just trying to take advantage of me."

She did slam the receiver down at that, and returned to the kitchen. The meal had been mostly demolished, and Edmund was eyeing her plate of scalloped potatoes, which were becoming cold and soupy.

"Who is it?" Belle said indifferently.

"It was Mr. Bernic. He wants me to go out with him tonight," she said a little wearily. "I wonder whether Mr. Bedlington is not coming to supper."

"Lucky he didn't," laughed Belle.

"Belle and me are going to the movie tonight," said Bill.

The 'phone rang again, Mrs. Cristi rose hastily and was gone, though Belle bounced, her chair scraping.

"Hello, hello!" Mrs. Cristi sat down at the chair beside the 'phone. Her long back was straight, even arched inward as she leaned forward. She made a movement as though adjusting her hat.

"Bernic speaking. How are you tonight, Mrs. Cristi?"

"Oh, take me away from all this!" She laughed hysterically.

"That's just what I was about to propose. I'll call around from you with the car at about nine o'clock. Are you on?"

"Fine, Mr. Bernic. Come right away. Come at eight o'clock."

"No, nine."

"I say, no. Come for me at eight."

"But why so early?"

"Come at half after eight, anyway."

"Oh, say dearie, what's the rush, won't nine do?"

"Better come at half after, if you want to find me here. Now remember. I won't be here at nine."

"Won't be there? Say, are you double-crossing me, or what?"

"Never mind. I'll be all ready at eight o'clock, but I won't promise for nine."

He laughed.

"Well, alright. I guess I can make it alright. I'd like to come at nine, though, just to see what you're putting over on me."

"But I said I wouldn't be here at nine."

"Alright girlie. Goodbye."

"Who was it this time?" asked Belle suspiciously.

"Oh, he wants me to be ready a little after eight. You'll have to stay home from the show this time, since Lida is going out, and look after the house. Bill won't mind, will you, Bill?"

"Oh, no!" groaned Bill. He would have a good enough time, rough-housing about with Belle and the kids, chatting with such roomers as appeared, lunching with Belle—until twelve or one when his landlady re-appeared. But he had spent so many nights that way. A little change would have been acceptable.

"Oh, Mother, have I got to stay home again tonight? Why don't you have your heavy hero take us all in his car? No, of course he probably doesn't want to hold a party." Belle's clipped swift accents were as rapid as her mother's. Her mother did not have to say anything.

"Oh no, that wouldn't do at all," said Baby satirically. "Mother couldn't vamp him then."

Mr. Bedlington And Belle

Belle was sober for a few minutes after the bill-collector from McCready's had called at nine o'clock. Though she insisted that her mother was out, the man ignored all that, and spoke as though she were responsible. What was going to be done about it? She wondered, herself. Her mother wouldn't pay them anything, and the man would simply be back again, perhaps tomorrow night. What a life! Oh well, she and Bill would go out tomorrow night, and she'd certainly see to that.

"It's time you kids went to bed," she announced suddenly, lifting her face from her hand and rising suddenly from the chair at the 'phone in the hall where she had sunk upon the man's departure. Bill was up in his room for the duration of the interview.

"Aw—Mamma ain't home. I won't go to bed," wailed Edmund from the stair banister, where he clung to the oak newel post as though to the neck of a flying-maned horse. Baby sat on a lower step, where it curved around the post, and so out of the way of anyone passing up the stairs or down, sewing a dress for her doll—she still had one indestructible doll. She had been trying to complete a shawl from her mother's Christmas, but it had become tangled and dirty, and Belle was too busy tonight to help her—though it was a good time, when her mother was out.

"Lucky thing for you Mamma isn't home," said Belle. "And don't say ain't. It makes you sound like a Yankee."

"Mamma ain't home," crooned Edmund. "I don't want to go to bed till Mamma gets home. I want to wait up for Mamma."

"Well, you're not going to," said Belle sternly. "Isn't he just a terrible boy," she adjured Ronnie and Albert, the two law students, who were ascending to their room.

"That's right, little boys should go to bed early," they snickered.

Belle, having employed a modicum of blandishment, seized Edmund under the arms and hoisted him from the banister. As she carried him upstairs he began to howl.

"Mother says you're to sleep in the back room tonight," she told him. "Belle's going to fix everything up nice for you. Come on, Baby, you too."

"Have I got to sleep there too? I won't do it. I'm going to ask Mother what she means—"

"Why, I'll sleep there too, silly, with you," said Belle. Baby did not know just what to say to this. Still, she might wait for her mother. She was sure Belle couldn't make her go to bed if she didn't want to go.

Their night clothes were in the little backroom, the bedding was turned down, and everything had been arranged for them. It looked cute, as though their mother had done all this for them herself.

When Bell was free she closed the door on the children and went to the stairs leading to the third floor. There was no sound above. She was about to go up, to tap on Bill's door, when the house rang with the sound of the doorbell. She skipped down to answer it. You never know who it might be. That was one of the charms of keeping a rooming house. She rattled down the stairs. She dashed into the parlour and turned on the phonograph, then back to the hall to answer the door, to brisk measures.

The instant she touched the door-knob, it pulled off in her hand.

She called through the door window, laughing. "Turn the knob, will you, the knob's fallen off on this side. It does that sometimes." She clicked the lower latch, which had been set to keep the door locked.

The knob was slowly turning, and a bushy head, or rather a bushy beard below a black hat, appeared, and stared up at her a second. Then the door was opened, and the figure entered. Behind it came another, a woman dressed in a black, elderly way.

In heavy tones and a foreign accent the first figure announced:

"I am Dr. Calambroso. This is Madame Calambroso. We would like to look at some rooms if you have any such to rent."

"Yes, certainly, just step this way, will you?" He's a doctor, they'll be particular, she thought. But she hesitated in the hall. Which room should she show them? There was the big front room where Bill and Edmund had broken the chandelier that afternoon, and there was the one above it on the third floor. Then there was the room her mother had rented to that girl in the afternoon. She couldn't very well put them there. She would take them to the good front room.

In silence they trundled up the stairs and past Mrs. Cristi's room to the front. They all gazed about the large room, eying windows and marble fireplace.

"Nice large room," murmured the woman. "I'm afraid it would be too dear—"

"No, not too large for us, I think," boomed the Doctor.

"Yes, it's quite a large room," agreed Belle cordially. "And you see it's right in front, and second floor. It's really the best room in the house."

"How much would it be?" asked the man.

"Did you just want it for tonight?"

"No, we want to live here or wherever we take our room, at least."

"Well, I don't think Mother would let you have it for less than seven dollars a week."

"No." The Doctor shook his head. "I don't want to spend so much as that. Income should be scientifically apportioned, in my opinion. For this kind of temporary accommodation the percentage should be low."

"Well, let me see," said Belle. It was a strain not to think aloud. "We have one small room on the second floor at the back we could let you have quite cheaply and we're building a nice little veranda to it. You might like that one. Only my little sister and brother are sleeping there tonight—just for tonight because we're rather full up. Anyway"—decisively—"you'd better take a look at it, maybe you wouldn't like it at all." Belle's blue eyes shone candidly.

"Yes, we might look at it, I suppose," said the Doctor. His wife and he trundled after her along the hall, past Mrs. Cristi's room and the absent Miss Campbell's room and the bathroom, to the room where Edmund and Baby were sleeping. Belle tiptoed in, turned on the light, and began to talk in hushed tones. Edmund woke up, stared mystified at the strangers a moment then turned his head away from the light and went to sleep again.

"Yes, we would like to have the room. Of course it wouldn't do though, to—perhaps—you couldn't, perhaps, put us up anyway some other place for tonight?"

"Why—I'll fix that in a jiffy."

Belle took them downstairs to wait in the parlour, and came upstairs again to move the kids into the front bedroom. It was a wailful business, and while she was doing it she wondered whether it would not have been just as well to put the Doctor and his wife in the front room for one night. Then they might have rented it permanently. Too late to do that now. You've got to have your wits about you running a big house like this. Why couldn't her mother have been home?

"Bill!" she called lustily. "Bill?"

"Eh?" enquired Bill from his opened door.

"Come on and help get the kids moved."

"Good Lord, ain't they to bed yet? When did that Dunner fellow go?

In four strides, Bill was down to the second floor beside her.

"Oh, long ago. Go to the back room and get the kids' bed-quilts. Hurry up. There's a man and woman waiting for the room."

Bill gaped at her, and went down the hall for the quilts. He took the other bedding in for the waiting couple while Belle got towels from the linen closet. Then he went and sat patiently on the landing above while Belle went downstairs for the bearded one—she was calling him "Doctor" already—and his wife. She explained that the bathroom was right next to their room, and nicely hoped that they would have a good night. Bill began to fidget.

At last she came to the stairs, and he muttered:

"Come on up and sit on the steps. Nobody is up here."

She ascended softly and sat beside him. They did not say much but they were having a good time. Occasionally, there was a giggle or a squeak. Their faces were luminous and glowing in the half-light. Before many minutes had passed they heard the front door click and then bang shut.

"Keep still," said Bill. "It's just Lida coming in."

They were quiet for a while and the person seemed to go back to the kitchen. Then it came upstairs. Belle began to wriggle. What was she to do? Perhaps it would go into one of the rooms, and then she could slip down.

"It's Mr. Bedlington," she whispered.

"Like hell," said Bill. "Come on to my room."

She half rose then sat down again. "No."

Then the steps came to the hall, went down the hall to the back room where the Doctor and his spouse were. They heard the knob turn, then a groan and a timid, "I—I'm sorry!" Then the steps went back to the stairs, paused thoughtfully. They began to ascend toward the third floor instead of going down again. Bill gripped Belle's

37

wrist, and held her from trying to run away. If he'd let her run downstairs, Mr. Bedlington might not catch on at all. She struggled to her feet just as he came around the corner and saw them.

"Oh, it's you, "said Mr. Bedlington.

"Nice evening ain't it?" said Bill.

"I want to talk to you, Belle," said Mr. Bedlington. "Come on downstairs."

"Think I'll go to my room," said Bill significantly.

"Yes, Mr. Bedlington," said Belle. She stepped heavily on each stair tread behind thin shoulders.

"Belle," said Mr. Bedlington when they got to the lower hall. "I want you to keep away from that third floor. I don't want you to go up there at all." He was looking at her thoughtfully and differently than he had ever looked at her before. She did not know what to say.

"But why? What's wrong about it, Mr. Bedlington?"

"Just because I wish it," said Mr. Bedlington. She hadn't known that he could be so firm.

She tossed her head. She didn't know why the third floor should be different from the others. She was going to tell him this when a thought struck her.

"Oh Mr. Bedlington! There was a man to see Mother, just a minute or two ago. I was putting the children to bed." (Mr. Bedlington's expression hadn't improved yet). "He was from the store where we get out groceries. He says there's a big bill run up. Isn't that awful? I'm sure he'll have his lawyer write us a letter."

"Have you been ordering your groceries on a charge account?"

"Yes, but my goodness, Mother thought they would give us some time to pay it, or why order that way?"

"You can't expect stores to give credit forever," said Mr. Bedlington. "They have to have their money, the same as anyone else." He sounded grim and different from the way he had been before. She wondered whether she could get around him.

38

"Yes, but they ought to have a heart, Mr. Bedlington." Belle made large eyes. "I wonder if they'll try to take our furniture away from us."

"They might try, if you can't pay. Well, it's too bad. What does your mother do with the money she gets?"

"Why Mr. Bedlington, I don't know. Really, she's the strangest woman," said Belle, starting on a new tack. "She doesn't have much money you know, and she had so many expenses. But I often wondered just how she spent the money every week myself."

"You'll have to manage differently after this. You'll just have to take hold of things and manage yourself, Belle. You're a smart girl. You can do it, but your mother wasn't cut out to be a rooming house keeper, I don't think. There's lots of things you could do to make things better. I don't think that dress you have is a good one to answer the door in." He glanced at the sleeveless cotton chemise top, and blushed. "People come to the door for rooms, and if they are particular, when they see an untidy looking person answer the door they're discouraged and they go away. I know you don't mean to be untidy, Belle."

"They might think I was the second parlour maid," giggled Belle. "But Mr. Bedlington, how can I buy a dress? I can never get any money."

"Well, I'll lend you the money to get a little dress that you can answer the door in."

"Oh, I say! That would be lovely, Mr. Bedlington. You're a dear."

Mr. Bedlington had a dazed look, then he blushed hotly.

"But you must do as I say if you want to make this house pay. And you mustn't go up on the third floor." He paused. "You're a smart girl, Belle. If you'll just be a good girl, and be careful, you can do so much, and everything will work out all right." He was talking as though things were going to the cogs now. Belle became serious.

"Yes, but there are all these debts coming in—I mean—"

"There aren't any others, are there, besides the grocer?"

"Well—I don't know—I guess that's all there are now."

Mr. Bedlington drew a long breath.

"Well—if you're sure that's all—I'll pay this bill, Belle. But you keep tab on things after this, and don't buy anything you can't pay for without telling me, will you?"

"Well, I guess not! I'm going to be just as careful from now on!"

Mr. Bedlington smiled shyly. "I guess that's all. I was going to sleep in the back room on the second floor, so that I could work on my veranda without disturbing anybody, but if you've rented it, so much the better."

"Oh, yes, I rented it. I guess they'll be staying permanently. He's a doctor. Say, Mr. Bedlington, what kind of a dress would you want me to get?"

"Oh, I should think something quite nice, but not too fancy to work in. Something pink, that would match your cheeks," he said playfully. "You know the right kind better than I do. I'll leave it to you, Belle."

"I suppose I'd better get it right away."

"I'll give you a blank cheque tomorrow. You remind me of it." Mr. Bedlington turned away. "Goodnight, Belle."

"Goodnight. You—you're so good, Mr. Bedlington!"

He was halfway upstairs, and pretended not to hear. Outside the Doctor's room stood his suitcase with clothing protruding from it, and a bundle of bedding. He picked them up and went into the front room and turned on the light. There in the bed were Baby and Edmund, sleeping peacefully.

Mr. Bedlington turned off the light and tiptoed up to his old room at the third floor back. As he closed the door he remembered: he wouldn't be able to keep an eye on Mrs. Cristi. He wouldn't even know when she came in.

Mrs. Webster

At about seven o'clock, Mr. Bedlington slipped out of the house, after eating a dish of shredded wheat at the kitchen cabinet, and leaving a blank cheque for Belle on the table. He patted the envelope full of cheques for his plasterers and carpenters in his pocket. As he went out to the veranda he drew a deep breath. It was a great day for work, inside at least. And if the weather would break, they might be able to do some outside jobs too.

No one else seemed to be up, though there was a sort of premonition stir throughout the house, as though the occupants of the rooms were wondering whether they wanted to rise and face the day ahead of them. A few minutes later, Bill came softly down the two flights of stairs, grabbed a couple of cookies remaining from Mr. Bedlington's breakfast, and went down the steep steps to the basement, where he shook down the furnace and threw on shovelful after shovelful of hard coal. A shelf extended along the wall, covered with tools new and old, paint tins, rags and bottles. Flakes of whitewash had fallen from the ceiling to the floor.

The house was soon singing with warmth. When Bill came up to the kitchen again, Baby was there, dressed in her dark school uniform. She seemed very nice and proper, and she wanted to know where Belle was. Belle was half asleep on the davenport in the front parlour with Lida, and when Belle was woken, she wanted Baby to run upstairs and turn on the water for her bath. Belle would be right up. Baby enquired who had been her servant last year.

"Aw, go on, Baby. The water's hot, isn't it? Bill's been down to the furnace hasn't he? You know I arranged your bed for you last night."

Baby turned up her nose and said nothing. But she went.

Belle bestirred herself almost at once, knowing that one of the roomers would get the bathroom if she did not hurry. And in fact the door was locked and the new doctor and his beard came out at last. Her water was still running into the tub and out of its overflow. She climbed in and found that she had no soap and no sponge.

"Baby! Baby! Come here."

"What's the matter with you?" screeched Carlotta from downstairs.

"What?" asked Belle. She couldn't hear for splashing the water.

"What?" asked Baby.

"Baby! Bring me some soap and a sponge. I forgot them."

"What did you forget them for?" Baby was on the stairs now.

"Hurry up or I'll catch cold."

In a few minutes, Belle came downstairs, and things began to brighten. She put bacon and eggs on the stove for breakfast, and got Bill and Edmund and Carlotta seated at the table. All began to munch shredded wheat. The milk was cold and the cream clotted with ice. Nobody bothered about Mrs. Cristi, who always slept in; and it was not nice to awaken Lida early when she had been out the night before. There was whistling on the top floor where the students were shaving, and their mother called them to breakfast. Lida soon appeared. Baby left for school. The doctor and his wife and beard went out and were back before you realized that any time at all had passed. The morning was slipping along smoothly.

Lida was sweeping the stair carpets. She did not have any

stockings on. Belle, wearing the satin dress with the cotton chemise top, paused her with a pan-full of hot water to scrub the floor of Miss Campbell's room.

"How did you and your dentist get on last night?"

"My Everett!" said Lida screwing up her eyes. "I'm crazy about him. No kidding. Says we're going to get married and he'll take me to California. They have oranges and everything down there. Just think, wouldn't it be a swell place to live? Oh gee Belle, you don't know how I love Everett."

"That's where they make the movies, too," said Belle. "Maybe he'll get you into the movies, eh?"

"Oh, I don't care for the movies. I'll be happy enough without them."

"Well, it's your funeral. If you want to get married, go ahead."

Belle was just emptying the pan of thick water in the bathroom when Miss Campbell arrived in a taxi with her belongings.

As soon as the taxi-driver had brought the last suitcase into the hall, Belle and Bill began helping to carry the luggage up to Miss Campbell's room. Miss Campbell was delighted with everyone's easy cordiality. She felt that she had come to a real home this time. The people had an interest in you, and they were so human and lively themselves! Contrasted with the usual rooming house, it was as different as night and day.

When she reached the room it looked only too familiar. The curtains had not been changed, and their filthiness was quite discouraged. She yanked down several large funereal landscapes from the wall, unerringly selected a bag, opened and plucked three small reproductions of modern paintings from it and hung them, then and there. Nor had the gas fixtures and the gas stove been removed. The floor around the carpet was still streaky and damp where Belle had scrubbed. Dampened herself by the total effect, Miss Campbell stopped Belle the next time she passed the door and began to question her. But there was a scream downstairs.

"Belle, the water!"

Belle dashed away into the bathroom whence loud splashing sounds emerged. There were churnings and jolts from a large pipe in the hall. The water in the bathroom would stop running while air escaped, and then start again explosively. Belle dashed back, damp and flushed.

"Mrs. Wells downstairs always gives the warning," she explained. "She can hear it first in the kitchenette. The hot water's connected with the furnace, you see, and when the furnace gets hot, the pipes begin to jolt. Then I have to let it run in the bathroom for fear something might burst."

The apprehension was vividly confirmed by the sounds of gurgling and hissing and thumping from all parts of the house. And when Miss Campbell went into the bathroom a little later she found the water still running, boiling hot, stopping and starting explosively, while the pipes groaned. Tears were streaming down the walls, the air was full of steam, and the windowpanes, which had been opaque when the water was first turned on, were now weeping too.

"That might happen in any house," she thought, already asking excuses for the special nature of this house and its inhabitants, though she had been reared in a home of five sisters and brothers. Until eleven o'clock she was busy arranging her belongings. Then she had to get to her pupils in Rosedale. She did not return till late afternoon, and there was no change in the disposition of the furnishings. She decided to see Mrs. Cristi about it.

When she knocked at the door of the front parlour, Bill called, "come in." Mrs. Cristi would soon be back, he told her. He himself was lying comfortably on the davenport, his head in his clasped hands. His eyes were the only things about him that moved. He said:

"That was a rather unfortunate introduction of ours yesterday. It might put you wrong."

"Oh, the electric light coming down, of course that was an accident."

"Oh, that! Well, I meant about Mrs. Cristi telling you I was from the South. Of course I am, but as a matter of fact I'm a Jew."

"An Irish Jew?" asked Miss Campbell, smiling.

"That's right! How did you know?"

Miss Campbell was a little confused. "Well, I was just joking. I didn't think there really were any Irish Jews."

"They do make a lot of jokes about us on the stage," admitted Bill. "But that doesn't keep us from being real."

"Is that true, though? Irish Jews. Just think of that."

"Yeah," said Bill lazily. "Seems funny if you're not used to it. I never think of it." He sprawled upon the lounge and looked at her speculatively.

"Have you been in this country long?" asked Miss Campbell.

"Pretty near as long as I can remember. Say, what kind of fur is that hat you had on yesterday? Belle said it was ermine, but I wasn't making any bets either way."

"It's white fox."

Bill told her about hitch-hiking through the States, and his adventures in out-of-the-way places; but Mrs. Cristi did not appear, so the girl returned to her room. There was no change in it the next day, nor the day after that. Miss Campbell decided to cut the Gordian knot, and explained that he would rather have a different room. They showed her the little front room on the third floor. She had a pint of milk delivered every morning, and took her breakfasts, and sometimes a lunch, or supper, in her room. The two law students had the next one, but they were quiet. At the back of the hall were Bill's room and Mr. Bedlington's.

Saturday, she came in with some groceries at three o'clock in the afternoon, and on reaching the second floor she heard voices in Mrs. Cristi's bedroom. The door was open.

"Oh, Miss Campbell! Miss Campbell! Come in a minute, won't you?" I'd like you to meet Mrs.... Such a charming girl," she added to 'Mrs...' in a whisper. "What was your name again?"

"Mrs. Webster, Miss Campbell."

Miss Campbell had a prompt, contagious laugh. Mrs. Webster acknowledged the introduction rather coolly. She was sitting on the side of the bed, wearing an old green house wrap, partly open and disclosing scanty undergarments and rolled stockings. Miss Campbell, who was very dark, looked incredulously at her white skin. Mrs. Webster's eyes sought the ceiling.

The two older women continued their conversation, agreeing whole heartedly about the terribleness of sickness.

"It's neuritis I have," said Mrs. Cristi. "Some mornings I can scarcely get out of bed. The pain is something terrible, of course, but if a person does actually take to sick-bed, they ask you what's the matter with you. And unless you have a broken leg, or tuberculosis, they have no sympathy with you. Absolutely."

"Not even then," affirmed Mrs. Webster. "They don't have any sympathy with you in any case. You would think that in the condition I am, some people would have some sympathy for me, wouldn't you? I can't walk around, I can hardly wait on myself, but people never seem to take that into consideration. They are just hard-hearted these days. They are so." She looked up as though through heavy spectacles, drawing her mouth and chin down. "Nobody loves a cripple," she concluded.

"Oh, I'm sure they do," said Mrs. Cristi, "though they may not show it." She rose. "Let's go into the side room and look at it again," she proposed. "Don't you think people sympathize with cripples, Miss Campbell?" she asked.

"Surely I do," returned the girl. "I hope you like it here, Mrs. Webster, if you decide to stay." As she went up the stairs she heard Mrs. Cristi explaining that they were one big family here.

The two women went into the room which Miss. Campbell had had, and Mrs. Cristi made the same promises she had made to Miss Campbell. Those two girls who had lived in the room had been terrible. They had said that they would stay permanently, and at the end of a month… But then you come into contact with all cases when you let your room. She knew a lady when she saw one, never fear, and she was sure that she and Mrs. Webster would agree perfectly.

"I'll bring you in an extra rocker, and I'll have those gas fixtures taken right out of your way, and fix the electric light at the side."

Mrs. Webster was looking doubtfully at the carpet.

"Oh, yes, and it might be possible to get a new carpet for you."

"I was thinking—the curtains."

"Of course, of course, Mrs. Webster, we'll wash the curtains right away."

"It's so much nicer when the room is all ready for a person to move in," said Mrs. Webster.

"Oh, well, don't you think about that," said Mrs. Cristi. "Of course we'll help you get settled, and put things around to suit you. I shall help you unpack myself when you move in."

"Well—well, that's most considerate of you." Mrs. Webster was won now, but still a little incredulous of such consideration. "You know in my old place the landlady was—oh, you couldn't believe how mean and sniffy she was. If I'd ask her for anything the least out of the ordinary, she'd—"

"We're all just one big family here, Mrs. Webster." Mrs. Cristi spoke in a warning tone, as though to let her know that no coldness of formality would be tolerated. She helped the old woman downstairs and out of the door, and down the stone steps to the sidewalk.

"Won't you let me call a cab for you, Mrs. Webster?"

"No, thank you. The streetcar is just around the corner. I'm not too good to ride in a streetcar," she said grimly.

"Very well," Mrs. Cristi said crisply. "Till tomorrow, then, Mrs. Webster. *Goodbye!*"

"Goodbye," said the old woman, moving away on her crutches.

On A Due-Due-Dewy Day

At half-past nine o'clock the next day, Mrs. Cristi and Belle went downtown. Mrs. Cristi held Mr. Bedlington's blank cheque in her purse. It was a fine winter's morning, the air sparkling clear, and no snow on the streets. They walked a block, and then waited for a streetcar.

It was a double-header that came quietly rumbling along. They sat down on a side seat, not going beyond the conductor who sat at the door midway, selling tickets and taking money. Mrs. Cristi turned her back on the person next to her and went on talking to Belle.

"This is just the nice time of day to go downtown. We'll be finished in time to have lunch in the Palm Room. It's so crowded when you have to shop at noon. All those shop girls and stenographers."

"But Mother," said Belle. "We can't do any other shopping, can we? Just the one cheque. All I want is the dress."

"Yes, we'll try to get a neat little frock for you. That's why we're going down. Wasn't it nice of Mr. Bedlington to think of it!"

"It's easy to get around him, though."

"Ah. We shall see what we shall see," said Mrs. Cristi. She spoke as though nobody had ever used the phrase before. She had an eternal, enigmatic charm for her daughter. Belle thought that nobody could be so distinguished and so easily formal as her mother, and nobody could always say the right thing, the briefly clever thing, which wouldn't even occur to anyone else, like her.

They came to a transfer point, passed the conductor in his judicial eminence, and went out. After a few more blocks they had reached Yonge Street and the department store. They were in a crowd of nice looking shoppers in a vast big room which covered the whole ground floor of the building. There was a strange light, made up of the reflected glitter of merchandise, and the electric lights on the cream-coloured pillars. The aisles were broad, and made of creamy marble. There were canals down which the people drifted, while the counters and stands of merchandise were islands. That is what the placards called them: "Isles of Opportunity." There were bargains in everything that day, it seemed. Belle did not know where to turn, she wanted to go exploring. Perhaps she could find something she would rather have than a dress. But Mrs. Cristi went up to a floorwalker and asked him where the ladies' dress—no, the misses dress department was. It was on the third floor.

They went into a large elevator. Three other women stood at the back, and a girl, hatless, who spoke to the elevator man. In a minute, the elevator was filled. A huge woman approached it in a series of bounces. The starter raised his hand and had the car wait. The elevator man said: "Stand well back, please. Well to the back of the car." Everybody shuffled, but there remained a solid row of people about a foot back from the door. The huge fat woman tried to squeeze into the row, but it held, and she bulged out beyond the door. The operator indicated an imaginary line, where the door would go, and it bisected her. She tried to fit into another notch. No good. She had to get out. She laughed a ringing laugh. "Better luck next time. I might fit next time," they heard as the elevator shot upward. A few permitted themselves giggles.

Arriving in the misses' dress department, they gravitated at once to the most expensive racks. There were party gowns, a few sport frocks, though it was winter. Belle felt wonderful. As she tried on dress after dress, she saw herself in so many different roles, from day to day, from shopping to tea to dance. And the clerk looked at her as though her very bigness and health entitled her to respect. She could hardly bear to pass by some of the frocks, but then the next one might be still nicer. Finally, her mother, the clerk, and she, herself, decided that a striking sleeveless gown, cerise chiffon with an oriental embroidery top and pin tucking black velvet skirt, was the dress for her. It was a bargain at twenty-seven-fifty.

Then there were a few little extras, like stockings and gloves. Mrs. Cristi arranged it so that she could pay it all with the one cheque, and get two dollars and a half for their lunch and carfare. "He can't expect us to get our lunch and things out of our own pocket when he sends us like this. I expect he'll be pleased when we show him what a bargain we got."

In the Palm Room, the orchestra was nice, but not loud, rather plaintive. The carpets thick, the service quiet and deferential. Mrs. Cristi behaved as though she were a queen, incognito, comparing the Toronto she saw here with European capitals. Belle was almost awed. She remembered that her mother had told of coming here frequently before they had left her father.

"Would you like to go to a movie matinee, Belle?"

"It would be nice, Mamma, but I've got my dress."

"Yes," Mrs. Cristi said hastily, "I've a great deal to do when I get home. Only it isn't often we're all ready downtown in time for a matinee."

"Besides, we want to have a little money left when we get home," suggested Belle.

"Oh, we should have got Baby some things. I saw some cute motor blankets…"

"And we'll be needing some groceries pretty quick."

"Oh, Belle, don't be so—sordid and common."

"Well, anyway, I think we should have a nice supper for Mr. Bedlington."

As they were leaving a clock presented itself.

"We'll be home by two o'clock. I feel as though we'd been away a week," said Belle. Home seemed alluring and full of possibilities. What would they say to her new dress?

Curling Irons And Irony

One evening, Belle knocked at Miss Campbell's door, and said in her hushed tones, looking earnest with a slightly lowered head:

"Oh, Miss Campbell, have you curling irons? Ours are burnt out. Would you lend us yours? Be *right* back, soon as we're done with it."

Three mornings later Miss Campbell knocked at Mrs. Cristi's door, which, was half opened. She could see Belle and Bill lying on Mrs. Cristi's broad bed, on their backs, their arms entwined, laughing, and watching Mrs. Cristi who was standing before the dresser in a mauve princess slip, low at the top, and even shorter than her dress skirts. Her long arms looked long as weather-vanes and she was doing her hair, putting on her rouge. About the room played Baby with a teddy bear. She would knock it a couple of yards with her fist, then pounce on it and say: "You'd run away from me, would you? Well, you won't." Edmund was spinning a top nosily on the lid of a syrup pail.

"Come on in, Miss Campbell, come right on in," Belle called.

"I thought I'd like to have my curling irons, if you're finished with them." Expedition seemed to be the best rule of this call.

"Oh, that's alright, Belle's finished with them," said Mrs. Cristi.

"Belle, you should have taken them back. I never curl my hair." Her fading blonde hair was done in a patrician manner, straight back, with a coil low at the nape. She began rubbing rouge into her skin, and talking. "You never use rouge, do you, Miss Campbell?"

"Well, yes, of course. I'm glad if you can't notice it."

"It must blend beautifully, because we wouldn't know it, would we, Belle? But then you're so dark."

Belle and Bill had clenched their inner arms and were wrestling. Mrs. Cristi continued to rub in the rouge, as though she expected to make it form part of her cheeks. Miss Campbell saw her irons on the dresser, but Mrs. Cristi insisted on entertaining her for a few minutes. Beside them stood a coloured hunting picture—a woman in red hunting clothes standing alongside a chestnut horse, with a pack of brindled hounds about her high patent-leather boots. Mrs. Cristi saw Miss Campbell looking at this picture, and gestured toward it. It was one of those possessions of her very own which gave the place an air.

"My husband," she observed, "is an English gentleman. You know what I mean. High walls around the house, and hounds and borzoi dogs, but he was frightfully close, you know, he came to this country. The quarrels we had over one pair of boots I got. I paid thirty dollars for them. Had to, you know, to get the kind I wanted, for riding. But he didn't like it at all. I used them for hikes in the country, too."

"They served a double purpose, then," smiled Miss Campbell.

"But you know—men," continued Mrs. Cristi. "Miss Campbell, you just take my advice. Never marry. Never marry no matter if it's the Prince of Wales. Never get married. It's just bondage."

"Now candidly, Mrs. Cristi, did you feel that way before you got married?"

"Well, of course, I didn't know what men were like. No girl does. It's a shame. Belle never will get married if I can prevent it."

Mrs. Cristi spoke with decision and calm, insofar as she was ever calm. Her utterance was nearly always breathless and urgent as though she were enacting on the stage a scene of profound and tragic import.

"And didn't you like it at all in the country?" Miss Campbell pursued.

"It would be nice if Mr. Cristi would fix things up. I'm sure. I made the best of things. He used to keep a lot of men to work the farm, you know, and I had to get their meals, with only one maid. The men were all nice, though, they used to call me 'mother', and they used to sleep in the barn... Baby, have you been playing with my earring?"

"I suppose you had a lot to look after."

"Yes, but the men were so nice about everything, I didn't mind. I used to get the grandest meals for the Threshers. But Mr. Cristi didn't like it if I did anything for them. He was just plain jealous, that is the truth."

"That seems to be one of the great disadvantages of married life, doesn't it? The men get jealous. At least I've often read of it in novels."

"All he cared about was his hounds and his horses and his— ivied walls."

"Well, that seems to be the way. There's no satisfying them," asserted Miss Campbell, as though she knew all about matrimony from old time. "I guess I'll take my curlers now, Mrs. Cristi." She did not look at Belle and Bill.

This was the beginning of a long series of confidential chats. Mrs. Cristi had made up her mind that her little dark roomer was a clever little thing, who could be treated as an equal. Miss Campbell's flair for sympathetic attitude aided her in getting acquainted with everyone in the house. The first time Mr. Bedlington took her into his confidence, for example, he happened to be working in the basement, sawing boards to build his veranda off the second storey back room. Miss Campbell had taught her pupils in Rosedale that day wearing a blouse with chiffon sleeves, because her tailored white blouse was dirty, and she felt, she told herself, like a fool. She swore that her tailored blouse would be washed that night, or she would know the reason.

Mr. Bedlington was a shy man, but his dealings with a variety of people had made him adept in attempts to conceal it. Besides, he was really friendly. So there was no difficulty in getting to know him.

"Will these shavings and sawdust hurt your washing?" he asked.

"Oh, no, I'm just washing out the one blouse, and I can hang that in my room. It will dry nicely there. They keep the room so warm here, don't they?"

"Yes," said Mr. Bedlington. "They surely do use up the coal. I think if I were running the house I could keep it comfortable without burning quite so much coal. I don't like to find fault, because they've leased the house from me, and they can burn as much coal as they like, of course. But I think they're extravagant in some ways."

Miss Campbell smiled at his mild expression. He did not say, though she guessed, that it was their extravagant ways which had made him come there to live in the first place. Nor did he so much as hint that they had not paid their rent and that there was no certain prospect that they ever would pay it.

"Mrs. Cristi is such an interesting woman, don't you think?" went on Miss Campbell.

"Yes," said Mr. Bedlington, closing one eye to look down a board he was planning. 'I really think," he added softly, "that if Belle could be given an education she would make quite a woman...quite a woman. Belle's a nice girl. Quite a nice girl."

"Yes, I like Belle," agreed the girl, carelessly. "She's so—well, healthy and lively."

By this time she had her blouse washed, wrung out, and rinsed.

She took it upstairs to dry.

"Well, goodbye," said Mr. Bedlington. "We must have another talk some time."

"Surely Mr. Bedlington."

Moving In

When Miss Campbell reached the upper hall, she found that Mrs. Webster was moving in. One trunk stood on end in the hall, while another was being carried upstairs by two sweating storage hands, with Bill's guidance. Bill went on ahead carrying an old telescope bag. Mrs. Webster's gaze followed them anxiously. She wanted to be in the room when the luggage arrived, but she could not very well pass them on the stairs. She had to mount behind, very ponderously with her crutches.

She was exhausted from the day's excitement, breathless and weak. There was no sign of Mrs. Cristi or Belle. She felt it terribly to be old and on crutches and forced to live in one room, but she couldn't get on with either of her two daughters very long.

The men were panting and waiting for her to pay them when she reached her room. They gave her scant civility because they were sure that she would give them nothing above the regular charge. Finally, they were gone, and she sank down on the bed, in the midst of her luggage, while Bill went downstairs for her birdcage. She got her breath and greeted the canary: "Birdee! Birdee! Tweet—tweet!" while Bill went away leaving the door open.

Mrs. Cristi came in, wearing a blue suit, a smart shirtwaist with a bow tie, and her hat and earring.

"Oh, Mrs. Webster! I'm so sorry! It was stupid of me to be ill all day. I couldn't get the room cleaned as I promised. I did tell you, didn't I, that I'd have it all fixed up for you? Ah, I thought I did. Well, nothing has been done to it, except that Belle fixed up the bed and a few things like that that had to be done."

"Well," said Mrs. Webster, "well…" She felt too tired to cope with the situation, too old to match this fresh, tall woman who had the nerve to wear rouge. She must get to bed at any cost. "I really expected it would be all fixed up ready for me.…"

"Baby, come here," called Mrs. Cristi.

Baby came, and stood in the doorway, regarding the two women darkly with her chin down.

"Put the kettle on. Make Mrs. Webster some tea. Mrs. Webster you let me help you get your things off." Baby vanished, wordless.

Mrs. Webster sighed. There was a terrible speed about everything Mrs. Cristi did and said. Mrs. Webster rose stiffly. She was a large woman with immense hips and bust, with a small, old-fashioned drawn-in waistline. It was very different with Mrs. Cristi, whose waist was about the same size as Mrs. Webster's, but who measured nearly the same all the way up and down. She had the modern girlish figure, except that her knees were stiff, and her ankles noticeably thick.

Baby came into the room with a nice smile and a tray with tea things.

"That's exceedingly kind of you, my dear," said Mrs. Webster.

"You're very welcome, Mrs. Webster!" sang Baby in a nicely modulated voice. The old woman thankfully took a sip of tea, and bit off a piece from one of the cakes, talking all the time of old age and her daughters. It was strange how daughters changed after they had left home and got married.

"Don't you ever forget your mother when you grow up, Carlotta!" said Mrs. Cristi. "I know you never will."

Mrs. Webster wagged her head, and took another drink of tea.

She knew Carlotta would.

"But I'd rather die than see you ever to get married," said Mrs. Cristi. Baby muttered something that sounded like, "Do what I please when I'm big!"

"Well, I wouldn't go so far with stipulations as to tell a girl she couldn't get married," the old woman objected. "But I don't think they should go so far as to forget their mother altogether. My, that tea tastes good, when you're a little tired."

"Sure you won't have anything more?" asked Mrs. Cristi. "I hope you rest well, Mrs.... If there's anything you want, you know, don't be afraid to ask, and we'll be glad to do anything. You bring the things, Baby. Goodnight."

"Goodnight, Mrs. Webster."

"Goodnight."

As soon as the voices had gone downstairs, Mrs. Webster took up her crutches and hobbled to the bathroom. The door was half-open. Belle was inside, washing. Mrs. Webster excused herself profusely, embarrassed.

"Come in. Come right in, Mrs. Webster." Belle spoke cordially. "Don't mind me. I'm just washing."

Mrs. Webster might have suspected as much, for Belle was vigorously soaping her arms and scrubbing them with a scrub brush. The old lady wanted neither to go away nor to stay. Belle told her that the winter was setting in early. "But you'll be lots warm here, alright. We always keep a good fire on, and lots of warm water. Let me help you."

When she returned to her room, Mrs. Webster opened her bed. First to meet her eye was a dirty pillowcase, which she removed, spreading a cloth of her own over the pillow. There were quilts on top, and one underneath which was especially heavy, so she turned back the others and looked at it. It was a patch quilt, made of men's suiting and overcoat material, and tied with red yarn. Between two layers of this there seemed to be a filling of cotton batting. It was so heavy she could hardly lift it. Rebelliously and deliberately she dragged it off. She wouldn't wear that, if she froze.

Then she looked at the sheets. They were soiled ones. She was filled with such horror and indignation that she could hear her heart going. Misgivings about the landlady and the whole establishment sprang into her mind. She went to the door in her nightgown and peeped out to see if she could find Mrs. Cristi. If she did she might tell her she was going to leave. She could hear the phonograph grinding and Mrs. Cristi talking on the 'phone downstairs, to some man, she was sure. She was telling him to come over right away, and he seemed to be teasing her.

Mrs. Webster locked her door and went back and crawled into bed, exhausted.

Baby Visits Daddy

Sunday was a dull day in the Cristi household. It was only in the evening that things began to take on a tinge of interest, much less romance. Sunday morning Mrs. Cristi managed to sleep even later that usual, particularly if Belle had agreed to bring her breakfast in bed. The roomers stirred about vaguely, some sleeping, some taking baths, but mainly keeping to their rooms. Bill and Belle and the children carried on the house as usual, attending to furnace and meals. Mr. Bedlington put on a brown suit and a blue tie and went to church at eleven. Miss Campbell practiced typing in her room. Mrs. Webster read her Bible after getting her own breakfast. One of the law students went upstairs and studied, the other went tobogganing in the snow at Riverdale Park with a girl.

Before noon, Baby called up her father. Mr. Cristi's voice over the telephone always had a curious effect on her. She liked him so much better than her mother, with whom she was obliged to live, that she really made the latter uncomfortable for hours after such a conversation, with the way she looked, and the things she said.

"Hello, Daddy!" she shrilled.

"Hello Baby, that's you Baby, isn't it?"

"Yes, Daddy. I just thought I'd call you up today. It's Sunday. Do you want me to come out on the streetcar and see you?"

"Why sure, Baby. You–you aren't coming alone, are you?"

"Of course I am Daddy. Mamma doesn't want to come."

"Well… you might bring Edmund though," Mr. Cristi's voice suggested.

"I don't know, I'll see," said Baby hastily. "Maybe Belle won't let him come."

"Oh. Belle won't let him come. Does Belle want to talk to me?"

"Not that I know of."

"Well, I'll be glad to have you come out to visit me, Baby. He'll come if you can, what time are you coming?

"Oh, I'll get out on the three o'clock car. I'll start early so I won't miss it. The streetcars here in the city are awfully slow now, with the snow and everything."

"Alright, Baby."

"Alright, Daddy."

"Remember me to Mother and Belle and Edmund. Is everything going alright?"

"Well," Baby remembered the roomers. "Mother says it is, but I can't see it myself."

"Alright, Baby." There was a melancholy smile in Mr. Cristi's tones. "Goodbye."

"Goodbye, Daddy. See you soon."

"What are you hanging around for when I'm 'phoning?" she snarled at Edmund in one word. He had been leaning against the wall in the hall, watching her as she talked, and murmuring to himself, "Daddy, why don't you come here and see us sometimes… Daddy I want to come and see you." Now he asked:

"Can I go with you to see Daddy?"

"No you can't, I'm going alone. Why can't you keep still when people are 'phoning? I bet he couldn't hear a word I was saying."

A hopeful gleam lit Edmund's eye. "Do you s'pose he could hear me?… Aw-w, why can't I go with you?"

"It's too cold. Ask Belle if it isn't."

"Yeah, I know Belle," he whined. "She won't let you do nothing! I know Belle."

Considering this fact, their faces showed a remarkable degree of astonishment at the sound of her voice coming from the drawing room at the end of the hall—a shrill, incensed voice, quite different from that of the everyday Belle.

"You *would* write to another girl, wouldn't you? You *would*!" She was stamping her feet. The children were standing at the door. Bill was sitting at a desk, with a sheet of paper in his hand. Belle was tearing up the envelope. "There! And there! And there!" She stamped on each piece of the envelope as she threw it on the floor.

"Aw, Belle," said Bill. "Don't burn up about it! Anyhow, you never got the letter. I didn't put the letter in the envelope yet."

Quick as a flash she was on him.

"Didn't I?"

She snatched the sheets from his hand and began tearing them up. The action seemed to drive her into a steeper rage, and her voice rose again. "Oh, oh! Oh! You–you-villain! You dirty low fake, you! You would write to a girl, would you!" She stamped again, her lips white, her head shaking.

Bill did not laugh; he was sober as though he was afraid of her.

"You give me my letter back. Give it back, do you hear?"

For answer she stamped on the pieces.

"What right have you got to tear up people's letters? Tell me that!"

"I'd tear up a dozen of them," she returned. "I would!—you dare!"

Bill had reached out a soothing hand to her. It was no use getting mad now, the letter was destroyed—or only mad enough to neutralize her anger.

"You dare touch me, will you? Oh, you'd write to another girl, would you? Don't you come near me, you—you—" She shot to the door, never seeing the children as they stepped back from it. Bill followed her upstairs and into Mrs. Cristi's room. They could hear sharp and vague muffled noises.

"I guess Mamma won't let them fight," said Edmund.

"No, she won't let them fight," said Baby, going away to prepare herself for the visit to her father.

Edmund sat down on the ornamental curve of the stairway and began murmuring again. It was no use trying to get Belle or his mother to let him go now. They would pay no attention to him.

"Oh Daddy, why don't you come and see us? Aw Daddy, I want to see you so bad."

Mrs. Webster Mends

The Cristis were very nice to Mrs. Webster, so far as talking to her and listening went, but they did not do much for her in the way of service. The pillowcases remained, unwashed and unmoved, on the back of a chair for a week. She could not get clean towels without asking for them repeatedly. Yet the girls and Mrs. Cristi were always nice to her. She soon saw that a species of favouritism reigned.

In the matter of the clean linens and towels, for example. The boys, so Miss Campbell told her, got everything they asked for; their beds were made up and their rooms tidied and swept first thing in the morning. Later, if there was time, the girls' rooms were taken care of. And Mrs. Wells, as the mother of the boys, could get what she wanted. But the rest had to shift for themselves. Miss Campbell did not say that she did so by going to the linen closet—just across the hall from Mrs. Webster's room–and taking what linen she needed. Mrs. Webster would never think of that, she'd consider it stealing. So they imposed upon her.

One afternoon late Mrs. Cristi came into Mrs. Webster's room.

"Oh, I've been lying down most of the day," she replied to Mrs. Webster's query. "So-o wretched! I wish I were seventy like you, Mrs. Webster. I do really. I would be all over my worries, my children wouldn't bother me, men wouldn't bother me then, and I could be quite calm and settled. I'd just love to be settled now," she said, shaking her head convincingly.

But in the foreground of this major trouble was a problem of a dress. She carried it over her arm—a green velvet affair—with the back of the skirt and the arms wrinkled. She held it up to Mrs. Webster.

"Look at it!" she exclaimed. "Just look at it! What am I to do with it? *I* don't know what to do with it, and I've got to go to a dinner tonight. What shall I *do* with it?" she repeated, in a frenzy of horror.

Mrs. Webster examined the dress. The wrinkles were very bad, and there was a tear in one of the sleeves. Belle had been wearing it as well as her mother.

"Why, the only way you can fix that, is to put water over in your tea kettle and wait till it commences to boil. Then you take the lid off the kettle, and hold the dress over the steam, till you get it all well steamed, the press it, using a cloth."

Mrs. Cristi had been scarcely listening to her.

"Oh, I've never done that. I'm sure if I tried to do that I'd spoil it. It's so easy to ruin them. And I did want to go to that dinner so."

"Well, if you don't mind waiting," said Mrs. Webster mildly, "I'll see what I can do for it. I'll put my kettle on right away."

"Oh, that's so kind of you. Isn't it nasty to be held up that way because the dress you want to wear isn't ready?"

Mrs. Webster hobbled over to her trunk by the window, and turned on the switch to heat her electric toaster on the trunk. There was water in her little kettle, and she placed it on the toaster.

"Now, if you send me up an iron, Mrs. Cristi, I'll be all ready to press the dress as soon as I get it steamed."

"Thanks so much. I'll go down right now, Mrs. Webster."

In a few minutes, the little kettle was humming, and Mrs. Webster took off the lid and held portions of the dress to the steam. Before she had treated all of the wrinkled areas, Belle appeared with the iron and a cloth for the pressing, and told her how nice this was of her. Then Mrs. Cristi entered in her slip, well rouged, and with her hair arranged, earring and all.

"All ready?" she asked. "If I don't get away soon we can't get seats for the first show."

"I'm just ready to begin pressing," said Mrs. Webster, looking up as though from beneath spectacles. She smoothed the cloth over the dress, and touched the iron with a moistened finger.

"Oh, I'm sorry," said Mrs. Cristi, and went back to her room. In a little while she called from there, and Mrs. Webster answered her cheerily:

"Just starting the back."

Mrs. Cristi said nothing, but put on her suit and hat. When she was all ready for the street she came out into the hall and appeared at Mrs. Webster's door.

"I'm afraid I can't wait now. It's getting too late. I'm sorry to have bothered you."

Mrs. Webster continued pressing as though she had not heard, and Mrs. Cristi went downstairs.

An hour after the job had been completed Belle came up and asked for the dress.

"Your mother's gone out, has she?" asked Mrs. Webster cannily.

"Oh, yes," said Belle carelessly. "She's gone out to a little tea-dance at the Rendezvous. I might wear the dress myself. Thanks awfully, Mrs. Webster," she added kindly, from the door.

Still later Mrs. Webster, passing through the hall, heard Belle talking in decisive tones over the telephone:

"Oh, you'd better not come. Mother's just gone out to pay some bills and do some shopping. You call tomorrow night." The receiver clicked down with her mother's promptness.

Mrs. Webster shook her head solemnly at herself in the dresser mirror. The clock sitting on its top told her it was time to prepare her supper. She felt the need of it, after dealing with that frantic woman. But her arms were tired, and she lowered herself into a rocking chair and leaned her crutches against its sides.

Time passed quickly that way, and as well as in any other. Twenty minutes later she rose and walked to her closet. It was filled with house-keeping equipment. A clothespin bag hung on a doorknob, a washboard stood around the corner. There were tins and dishes hanging on other nails. She took down a pot and put some water in it. From the window-sill she took a plate of beefsteak she had had ground in the butcher shop. Part of this she put into the pot. Then she cut up a carrot and an onion and added them to the stew. A pot of tea and a jar of marmalade and cookies completed the meal. After she had eaten, she got out some mending and sat down, content to be alone, but ready to receive any visitors chance might send her.

Le Médecin Malgré Lui

Mrs. Cristi got on well with the bearded Calambroso and his wife. She enquired effusively regarding his welfare whenever she chanced to meet him, calling him doctor at every opportunity. As for his wife, she was a meek-looking woman with, however, a certain eye, and she did not stir much outside the little room at the back, unless she went outside. For the first few days, that was. Also during these first few days she kept her door constantly partly opened, so that not much of what transpired in the hall of downstairs escaped her. But she and Mrs. Cristi did not have much to say to one another.

Before a week was out, Mrs. Calambroso had got acquainted with Mrs. Webster, but the truth was that she could not very well have escaped getting acquainted with her. Mrs. Webster considered this other elderly woman had been sent by Providence to lighten her lot. They had imparted to one another vast slices of their personal histories, and those of their children, before two days of their friendship had passed. But there remained ever more to tell, and no morning or afternoon passed without a tapping on the door of the other and dropping in for a minute which stretched into and hour and a half, and if such a rare morning did come and pass, it was because they had met each other in the hall and talked there, or because Mrs. Calambroso had gone out.

Of course they talked about their respective husbands before they had talked of many other things. Mrs. Webster could scarcely remember the first years of her widowhood, but still the thought of her poor husband, dead in his prime, was enough to make her sad. As for Mr. Calambroso, though she thought him villainous looking, a cross between a patent-medicine man, an old clothes man, and a distinguished surgeon, Mrs. Calambroso's confidence soon placed him on a footing of everyday reality in her imagination. She learned that the Doctor liked sausages, and did not like burlesque shows. This eased the feeling she got when she would come upon him, standing, an enigma, in the hall, hands in pockets, eyes on the floor.

The confidence of the women, indeed, reached a point where Mrs. Webster learned that the Doctor was not really a doctor at all—though he knew as much, or more, than most doctors in his own line. He was really a dietician.

He was tired of Toronto, it appeared. He and his wife were planning to go to Hamilton, and take a house there of their own. This was a project discussed in detail before it seemed to enter anyone's head that Mrs. Webster might go along. Then she herself became taken with it, and all day long they would talk about the plan. Mr. Calambroso, however, did not enter into these discussions, though he seemed to lurk in the background as a sinister cloud from which showers of blessings were to come. He came and went, and eyed Mrs. Webster speculatively, his eyes aglitter in his bushy face. Always he bade her the time of day with appreciative politeness. Sometimes he would appear in the house, in the middle of the afternoon or morning, but he went straight, and almost furtively, to his room.

These developments took place in a few days and all told, the Calambrosos did not live in the Cristi ménage for more than two weeks. It came about that Mr. (not Dr.) Calambroso was not ready to pay the rent at the end of the first week. Since Belle had let them in that night, nothing had been said about the rent. When she did mention the subject to Mrs. Calambroso, Mrs. Calambroso did not know what the Doctor was going to do about it. It seemed that while they had been prepared to pay in advance, they had had recent reverses.

Two days later, Mrs. Cristi met him, addressed him as Doctor without surname, conveyed to him that both he and she were superior to merely monetary concerns, but that equally as a matter of course, some recognition was due obvious facts, such as coal bills, and income taxes.

The Doctor, however, with a decision equalling his own suavity, gave her to understand that he was momentarily unable to meet this particular demand. He was committed to a policy or retrenchment, in lieu of the fact that he was about to establish a house of his own. He wouldn't impose on Mrs. Cristi's good nature long, for he wouldn't be with her long. But later when things began to look up, he'd attend to this little bill and one or two others in one fell swoop.

Mrs. Cristi agreed in a practical tone that that was the sensible way to look at it. One shouldn't run one's self short just to satisfy the whims of a creditor who did not need the money. For her part she didn't care. Let it run on. Let the Doctor pay when he moved away. She was not one of those suspicious haggling people of the professional landlady type.

Meanwhile, Mrs. Webster was daily becoming more closely involved in these plans of the Calambrosos. She had a little money, she had informed them, enough to buy a share in a house. They could all live comfortably together and she would have a home. They would attend to all her needs, she would have nothing more to worry her; her daughters could visit her sometimes (this was her own suggestion) but she would feel independent of them. It would be a splendid arrangement for everybody concerned.

Then a little coolness came into the friendship of the two women as will happen. It should have been just a temporary matter, making them a little more formal in addressing each other for a few days. But other things intervened. Mrs. Webster let Belle confide in her more, though she did not approve of Belle. Belle told her, though how Belle knew was beyond Mrs. Webster, that the Doctor, besides being no Doctor, but a dietician only, worked in the mornings one week and in the afternoons the next, and that he only earned ten dollars a week. Obviously, it was not feasible to undertake the establishment of a home with the expectation of deriving most of the financial support from the Calambrosos. She told the girl all about the plan then.

Belle was filled with horror. The foxy schemers! Why, they'd get a poor helpless old lady away like that, and Lord knew what they'd do with her. Neglect her or starve her or worry her to death getting her to make out her will in their favour. You read about such things in the newspapers every little while. It was certainly lucky Mrs. Webster had talked to her about it. The old foxes! Why Mr. Calambroso could easily mix up one of his dietician dishes and slip a little something into it…

After this Mrs. Webster's coolness increased, though that of Mrs. Calambroso seemed to pass, and she would willingly have been friends again. And Mrs. Webster saw the two depart with their luggage, walking to the streetcar one snowy morning with a feeling of having escaped the calamity of her helpless old age. She thought: "Oh, if I'd gone with them!"

Fur Coat

Throughout November the winter had seemed to dally, hesitating to deliver a fell blow, or to manifest the unremitting acerbity to human life which might be ascribed to it. There had been mild days, rainy and even sunny days and the snowstorms which came were soon dissipated, with their precipitated residue, leaving the streets dry and clean. People had not noticed that it was time for winter, and they had not begun to feel discomfort. But with the first few days of December came the stormy weather, and the snow remained. Those who had been prophesying a late winter found that instead it was to be an unusually early one, in full strength before Christmas.

Belle did not like this sudden appearance of winter. She expected to get a new heavy coat in due course, but she did not have it yet, and was obliged to wear her old one, in which every seam, she thought, was visible. She had to have a coat. Mrs. Cristi admitted, in conversation with Mr. Bedlington that she needed one badly. The next night Mr. Bedlington brought them an evening paper with an advertisement of heavy winter coats—good value, he considered, for twenty-five dollars. Nice plain coats; perhaps Belle would like to have one of these?

Of course Belle thought they were awfully cute, and Mrs. Cristi agreed that they would be just the thing for winter. So Mr. Bedlington made out a cheque, for twenty-five dollars. He did not leave it blank this time, remembering how they had bought the French dress. Mr. Bedlington was wonderful. He blushed before the combined praises of Belle and Mrs. Cristi, afraid this time that Belle would say she felt like kissing him.

In the morning the two were quite excited when they dressed and went downtown. They did not talk much, and the same idea must have been stirring in the brain of each. They agreed that you could get a nice little coat for twenty-five dollars, but there was no law compelling them to get it where Mr. Bedlington's sale was being held. They'd better look around for a while, window-shopping, before they decided what they would buy.

They alighted from the streetcar at College and Yonge, and walked down Yonge Street, looking at coats in the window. Soon they came to a store which was holding a sale of fur coats.

"Let's look at these," said Mrs. Cristi. They did not look long before they saw one, a shaggy brown coat, which they thought would look well on Belle. It was priced at one hundred and fifty.

"Oh, Mamma," breathed Belle.

"We might as well try them on, anyway, child," said Mrs. Cristi. "We're not obliged to buy."

Inside the store, the saleslady was most polite. She knew quality English people when she saw them. The coat was becoming to Belle. It fitted Mrs. Cristi herself, as she found when she jokingly tried it on. In fact there seemed to be no other coat in the store which suited them so well. They had stumbled upon a real bit of luck when they saw that coat in the window. And they could have it for one hundred and thirty-five dollars, fifteen less than the sale price. They liked it, and yet…

What was the trouble then, if they liked it, the saleslady—Madame herself—asked. They talked for quite awhile, and it did not appear that there was any definite reason why they should not have the coat. They tried it on again, and there was still less reason.

Madame folded the coat and made to return it to the window, and there was no reason at all why they should not have the coat. So Mrs. Cristi asked, somewhat hesitantly, for she was really excited now:

"Could we buy the coat by paying twenty-five dollars down?"

"Surely," assented Madame. "Pay for it anyway you like. A hundred dollars down, fifty dollars down, or twenty-five dollars down. And the balance, twenty dollars a month."

"Oh very well; that will be alright, then. We'll give you a cheque for twenty-five right now."

"Very well," said Madame. "Just come this way," She was leading the way to her desk at the back of the shop, but Mrs. Cristi halted her, and drew the cheque ready-made out from her purse. She had endorsed it at home.

Madame hesitated, as though she might wish to make enquiries. But Mr. Bedlington's tight scrawl seemed to reassure her. Still she took Mrs. Cristi to her desk. There were certain papers to be made out and signed, when you bought things on time. Madame was very nice about it all. Belle looked on, becoming graver as these complications arose. You had to sign your name to papers, and the coat wasn't really yours until it was all paid for. You had to pay on such a date every month. Belle wondered whether they weren't getting themselves into a mess. But her mother carried it all off with a grand air and a monosyllabic manner. It was a nuisance, a silly formality, but it had to be gone through. Only a silly formality.

They soon had the coat. They wouldn't have it delivered. They wouldn't carry it. Belle would wear it, and have the old one sent. Madame called a clerk to attend to this and bade them good day pleasantly. Belle walked out of the store feeling like a combination of a princess and a cinnamon bear. She had never worn a fur coat before.

"But it's so *warm*!" she cried to her mother, in the streetcar.

"Of course," said Mrs. Cristi dryly. "That's what it's for. It won't be too warm in winter. You're inside now."

Then, "I wonder what Mr. Bedlington will say?" the girl wondered.

"Why, Belle, he hasn't any kick coming. We only spent his twenty-five. We're going to pay the rest ourselves."

"That's right, he can't say anything." Belle drew the coat about her. It was hers. "He wouldn't anyway," she added, with sudden confidence.

Mr. Bedlington Pays A Call

That night Mr. Bedlington, having heard that Miss Campbell had a cold, took up to her room a concoction of his own, liniment and lemon and melted Vaseline which he guaranteed would cure any cold before you could say "Jack Robinson." His benevolence accounted for a brisk assurance now overlying his diffidence.

"Well, in that case, I must try it," said Miss Campbell, smiling. "If it cures as quickly as all that, you'd better stay and witness the transformation. Won't you sit down, Mr. Bedlington?"

Mr. Bedlington came in, leaving the door open, and sat on the trunk beside the wall, and they began to talk.

"Don't take it right away if you don't want to. I know people don't like to have others watch them taking medicine. This is a bad time of the year for colds, isn't it? We didn't have time to get used to winter. Have you seen Belle's new coat yet?"

"No, I was out all day, and I haven't seen Belle yet."

"She went downtown and got a fur one."

"A fur coat? Belle will look fine in a fur coat. But it seems rather—extravagant though of course I don't know much about their finances."

"Yes. Extravagant," returned Mr. Bedlington moodily. "You know, Miss Campbell, sometimes I get so discouraged, I don't know what to do. When I was a young fellow, living with my folks, it used to be the same way. Then I got away and went into carpentering, building. But every once in a while I have to put down my tools and get away from it all. The last time was five or six years ago; I got so discouraged I had to go away, take a trip."

"How interesting! Wasn't the business going well?"

"No, I say discouraged, but that isn't quite the word. The business was doing alright, better than I expected. But I got so I didn't take any interest in anything, it seemed. Didn't care what I did the next day. It was all the same to me. I didn't care about anything. So I went away."

"How funny! Did you want to travel?"

"No, I can't say that I did. I didn't know just what I did want. I didn't want anything, I mean. But I thought I better go away for a while and have a change of scene. I went up north, into the mining country."

"Where men are men, eh?"

"Yes." Mr. Bedlington giggled meekly. "I didn't see anything I wanted to invest money in, but the trip did me all kinds of good. I came back sooner than I expected; I was so anxious to get at my work again."

"I suppose everyone gets fed up that way with their work. I know teaching bores me terribly sometimes."

"Yes, I suppose teaching must be kind of monotonous. Do you have many children to teach?—I know you don't teach in a regular school, do you?"

"No, I do governess work with a family over in Rosedale. The children are small of course. Hardly old enough to go to school. That seemed nice when I first started to teach. I taught a kindergarten class in a public school, and I liked it. But it gets so monotonous, and after being with them all day you get so your mind works as though it were a child's."

"Yes, it must be kind of tiresome, alright. Oh, everybody's got their cross to bear, that's true." He wagged his little brown face, sitting on the trunk, his feet not touching the floor, his clean-cut features smiling. Miss Campbell listened sympathetically, and he went on:

"It makes me so discouraged, though, to see the way things have been going on in this house. I don't see how they can expect to make it pay."

"Mrs. Cristi is gaining experience of rooming houses," said Miss Campbell facetiously.

"But you can't advise them," said Mr. Bedlington, in a whisper, with an expression of awe. "They do worse things everyday."

They heard Belle's robust voice as though it had been in the next room, talking to Mrs. Webster downstairs.

"Oh, Mrs. Webster, look at my hat. I can't very well wear that with my new coat, can I?"

"It just needs the band turned, and brushing. It's a very suitable, nice black felt hat," returned Mrs. Webster firmly.

"Oh, but I don't know how to turn the band," moaned Belle, "and—"

"Give me the hat," said Mrs. Webster's voice.

Miss Campbell smiled, and Mr. Bedlington shook his head. The girl reflected that he thought her callous, and that if he could have smiled at the Cristis, he would not have been such an easy mark for their scheme.

"Belle is a nice girl, though," said Mr. Bedlington. "If she could just have a different sort of upbringing, or even go to church..."

"Yes, well, they all say we are a combination of environment and heredity," agreed Miss Campbell.

"Would you—do you think you could go with me to the movies or some play some night?" asked Mr. Bedlington, tapping the floor with his toes.

"Why yes, I think so, Mr. Bedlington. That would be very nice."

The little man climbed off the trunk and stood up. He held out his hand to bid her goodnight.

"Don't forget," he said. "And be sure and take that medicine. I heard that Mrs. Webster had a cold, and I'm going to mix some for her."

The girl felt some compunction about going out after that, but she had a date. She took a sip of medicine, as she was leaving, and slipping down the hall she heard Mrs. Webster talking to Mr. Bedlington. She grinned.

The Taste In Her Mouth

When Baby got roused, she forgot herself. That was the case with all of them; when they lifted their voices and the hot words came. It was nearly nine o'clock in the morning and Baby should have been leaving for school, but she was lecturing her mother, who lay in bed.

"Yes, you *would* go out with other men. You go out with those big bums all the time. I'm just going to tell Daddy on you, that's what I'm going to do. I'll tell him the way you've been carrying on. You would go with other men, would you!"

Baby bent her black brows upon her mother and the words tore from her like arrows. She stamped her foot.

"I know all about your goings on. *I'll* tell him, if Belle won't. Yes, I know you!" Loathing was in her tone. "You *would* go out with men, and stay up all hours of the night in the drawing room, with the light out."

"Oh! Oh!" gasped Mrs. Cristi, hiding her eyes in the pillow. "Baby stop! You've been sneaking around in the dark, you little eavesdropper, and imagine you've seen something you haven't seen at all. Stop. You're driving me crazy. Stop! I—I'll murder you if you don't stop!" She moaned, but there was no stopping Carlotta.

"No, you won't murder me. You just wait till Daddy hears. He'll tend to this. You going out with men!" she added once more with infinite disgust. "And sitting up with them all night. I suppose you want to go to bed with them like you used to with Daddy."

"Get out of this room!" screamed Mrs. Cristi. "Get out quick. Leave me alone or I'll—tell Belle to come here. At once!"

"You just wait," sniffed Baby, retreating to go downstairs and get ready for school. "I'll tell him."

Mrs. Cristi wept awhile, and went to sleep. Belle peeked into the room in the middle of the morning, without disturbing her. In the middle of the afternoon she woke up, and called Belle. She had lunch in bed, and went to sleep again. She wanted to get up in the evening, but Belle wouldn't let her, and Baby wouldn't appear or even let her voice be heard. Mrs. Cristi dreaded Baby the more for lurking away. When the next morning came, she didn't get up. She wasn't accustomed to rising before she felt like it. And after a lunch in bed again, she drifted off to sleep.

Miss Campbell came in late in the afternoon, and Mrs. Cristi heard her passing in the hall.

"Come in, Miss Campbell. Come on in. I've been sick in bed for two days. Didn't you know?"

"I'm sorry you're sick. I didn't know what had become of you. I hope it wasn't staying up so late to let me in…"

"Oh! No! My goodness! That's nothing. Stay out as late as you like, it doesn't bother us. Stay out just as late as you please, my dear. I wish I were young like yourself. I really do."

"Why, I was envying you, in your mature life, at the height of your mental powers."

"Oh—h! I'm sick to death of this house. Sick of it! Nothing goes right. We send the washing out Monday morning, and the next day we find that half of it was forgotten, and we have to wash that in the basement. I'm sick of it all. And always the coal bills. And if I go to bed! My dear, if I go to bed everything in this house goes to rack and ruin."

"Yes, but you have the satisfaction of doing for your children and of being independent."

"I hate children! Miss Campbell, I hate them! I just hate the nasty little beasts. They torment me till I don't know what I'm doing."

"Now, Mrs. Cristi, you know you're only talking like that. You don't really hate them. You can't hate them," Miss Campbell spoke decidedly.

"Yes I do! I—hate—those—children. Baby, the little imp. She really must have a devil, as the Scripture says, Miss Campbell. She must. And Belle. Belle means well, but she's more bother… Her father used to ill-treat her, let her work in the field, and even he called her a big fat pig. But he wasn't so terribly far wrong. He had his own worries, after all," said Mrs. Cristi, subsiding from the frenzied vehemence of her earlier speeches, and even wiping her dry hard grey-slate-blue eyes.

"Yes, but you don't hate your children, Mrs. Cristi," said the girl firmly. "That's absurd. No mother hates her children."

"You'd think they didn't have a mother. You'd think I was just a servant maid made to wait on them." Mrs. Cristi began to cry hoarsely. A kind of coarseness came into her voice and her expression which the girl had not noticed before. The sobs tore their way from her, shaking her body and the bed. "I do, I tell you, I hate them. Oh! I'm going to get up. Nothing goes when I'm sick in bed. Nothing goes. I ought to be lying quiet if I'm ever to get well. I shouldn't be up a minute with my back in the condition it is. But do you think they'll let me rest here? Do you think they will! Why, I worry myself sick about the work. They leave all the responsibility to me, sick or well. The house is like a pig pen. And there Belle and Lida playing the Victrola. *They* don't care. It's all up to me. I will get up. I've got to get up. I'm just a servant for them."

But first she stopped talking altogether for a few minutes, while she gave way once more to strangling sobs. Miss Campbell wondered why the girls did not hear her downstairs, but they had the phonograph playing, "On a dew-dew-dewy day." She approached the bed and placed her hand on Mrs. Cristi's shoulder.

"Now, Mrs. Cristi, you mustn't think and talk in that way. The children don't mean anything. They're just happy and healthy, and you should be glad that they are, because they owe it to you."

The gusts of sobbing abated enough to let the woman say:

"No—you'd think—they didn't have a mother—for all they care. For all they care. Let me get up. I'm going to get up."

Miss Campbell stood back and watched her solicitously, while she rose and sat on the edge of the bed in one movement.

"I'm going to get up and give this house a real cleaning up, if it ever had one. I will so."

She jerked herself out of the bed and stood in a very long white nightgown composed of holes and network at least half an inch in diameter.

"Oh, what an unusual nightgown," said Miss Campbell appreciatively.

"Yes, isn't it odd? My mother-in-law gave me this as one of her wedding presents. Real lace. Don't you go away my dear; I want to talk to you while I'm dressing."

Miss Campbell turned away from the door, for which she had been headed, and strolled about the room looking at the pictures while they talked. Her hostess threw on a green evening wrap as a dressing gown, and drew undergarments beneath the nightdress and dressing gown. She hobbled about stiffly looking for stockings, from closet to dresser drawer.

"It's too bad to bother you with my troubles, my dear," said Mrs. Cristi, drawing on a stocking. "Everybody in the house is so nice. There's Mrs. Webster and Mrs. Wells. Don't you like Mrs. Wells, Miss Campbell? And then she has two nice sons! You really should see more of Mrs. Wells."

"Yes, Mrs. Wells seems nice," returned Miss Campbell guardedly.

"It's fortunate for the boys to have their mother right here to look after them and get their meals. Not many college boys are so well cared for away from home." She strolled to the dresser to look at the picture of the red-coated hunters with their dogs and horses and high patent leather boots.

"Yes, you should see more of the Wells'," said Mrs. Cristi in her nearest approach to humour. "By the bye, I was so disappointed in Dr. Calambroso. He seemed to be such an able man, too."

The girl smiled. "One should have thought he'd make a good doctor. He seemed to have a bedside manner, didn't he?"

"Yes, such types as one meets when one rents one's rooms! You never *can* tell. There! Now I'm ready, I'm going to give this house such a cleaning as it never had before."

"Well, I'd best be getting to my room and cleaning myself up."

"Ah, teaching children is such a delightful occupation!"

Miss Campbell laughed from the stairs. "You wouldn't think so sometimes."

Mrs. Cristi went down to the kitchen. No one was there, though it was after five o'clock. She could hear Belle and Lida discussing Lida's Everett in the drawing room. Baby and Edmund seemed to be in the basement.

"Carlotta! Edmund!" she screamed. "Come up from there, you're all black with coal dust!" Then she remembered her last meeting with Baby, and her heart nearly stopped. She would ignore it and give orders. Make everybody tow the mark. "Baby! Edmund! Come! Come up quickly!" She stamped her foot.

Edmund appeared on the stairs, round-eyed.

"Ain't you sick anymore, Mamma?" he enquired dubiously.

"I am sick, but I'm obliged to be up," she returned in clipped accents. "Come here. You're all coal dust."

"No I'm not, Mamma," he returned earnestly. And Baby, who had followed him upstairs, looked on scornfully. On the contrary, there were white flakes on the back of his dark jacket.

"Where did you get that whitewash? Have you been scrubbing yourself around the walls?"

"No Mamma," said Edmund, betrayed. "There was flakes on the floor where we was playing."

"Oh, I see. Baby, you go with him up to Mother's room, and brush yourselves off. Then come down here and I'll give you something to do. Where's Belle and Lida? Tell them I want them. Right away."

The children departed down the hall, and Mrs. Cristi surveyed the room. It had not been swept for several days, apparently, and the dirt had been ground into the linoleum. A scrubbing was what it would have to have now. She swept it hastily. The tablecloth was dirty and covered with similar dishes. The kitchen cabinet stood opened, with half-eaten food and empty opened tin cans strewn about its top. She turned the hot water tap at once, and filled a stew pan. She wanted to get at the floor scrubbing before the girls should come.

There was no rag or scrub brush, of course, so she went to the closet and took out a somewhat ragged tea towel. There was no ammonia or other cleaner, so she threw in a cake of toilet soap whole, and knelt down in the middle of the kitchen and began to scrub. She had only been at it a minute when she realized the vast amount of time and effort ahead of her. If only the girls would come. But she wouldn't ask them to do it.

Suddenly there was a stupendous, thunderous rattling, as though the house was coming down, it seemed to her startled senses for an instant. Then she realized that the sounds came from the basement. It was the coalman, shovelling coal down a chute. She had told him to come days before, but he of course had ignored the order till she was sick. Everything conspired to wreck her nerves. Everything. The uproar died down to a few coals sliding down the tin chute. Then it became a crash again, a roaring swift descent.

"Ugh!" she screamed suddenly. "Girls! Belle! Lida! Come here!"

There was a rush of feet and Belle was bouncing into the room.

"Why, Mother! Scrubbing the floor! I thought you were sick!"

"I was," said Mrs. Cristi suddenly quiet, going on with her scrubbing. "I am sick still, if that is anything to you. Of course it doesn't matter, *I've* got to look after things or this house'll go to rack and ruin. I can't see what you girls have been doing, but I suppose you've been too busy running the phonograph and talking about fellows to do any work. A pair of infatuate fools, the pair of you," she added, without looking up.

"Oh, Mrs. Cristi," said Lida. "Let me do that. You're not fit. I'm all ready." She rolled up her sleeves and her stockings were already off. In truth, she and Belle were almost dumbfounded by a certain new tone in Mrs. Cristi, a doggedness instead of the old devil-take-it attitude. They felt a vague alarm lest she should be like this all the time from now on. It would certainly make things uncomfortable!

"No, Lida, you go in the parlour and turn on some record that reminds you of Everett. And you, Belle, go downstairs and tell the coalman if he can't make less noise. I only want one tone this time. I won't put up with the noise anymore." The impressive force of her speech had been sadly minimized by it, and the girls looked, she saw, as though they hadn't half heard. Lida just stood there. Belle went downstairs.

"Go on," said Mrs. Cristi to Lida in a more familiar tone. "Go in the drawing room. Take a broom and a cloth to dust things. I can't expect to clean the whole house myself, I suppose, at this hour of the day."

"Yes, Mrs. Cristi."

"And see the hall is done too on your way back. If I finish here before you do, I'll do the hall," she added cunningly. Lida sped away, alarmed at her mistress' sudden martyrdom. Mrs. Cristi went vigorously on with the scrubbing. She was enjoying herself. She did as much in five minutes as she was accustomed to doing in half an hour. She became so taken with the idea of speed, of scouring the house in a couple of hours, that she even neglected the corners of the room. Her head cleared, and she felt better. She'd show them, she'd show herself what she was capable of. The clanging shovelfuls of coal were forgotten, then became harmonious in her ears. She could hear the coalman and Belle indulging in a loud flirtation, but she didn't mind. This house was going to get the best setting-up it ever had. "And I am the prime agent of its sanitary reformation," she told herself.

Laughter and song and slamming doors sounded upstairs, the hiss of Lida's broom in the hall downstairs, the clangour of coal and the snorting of horses from the basement and outside; it was all music in her ears. She was the centre of it all. She would show them. They would have to admit that mother made things hum when she cared to take it into her head.

On the stairs, Belle and Lida met in the execution of errands Mrs. Cristi had given them.

"Isn't she awful?" asked Belle confidently.

"She's so ugly; the taste in her mouth makes her sick."

Belle laughed. Lida nodded. "Yes, she is."

Bathroom Confidences

Mrs. Cristi and Belle had various little manoeuvres by which they managed to come on intimate terms with their roomers. In the case of the women and girls, one of their favourite mannerisms was to wait until the individual was in the bathroom, then one of them would knock on the door. The astonished roomer would open it if the knocking was persisted in.

"Oh! It's only me, Miss Campbell—or Mrs. Webster—I just wanted to wash out these things in the bathtub, if it won't disturb you. Do you mind?"

Of course the roomer did not mind, and there ensued a heart-to-heart talk, exploiting the habits and likes and dislikes and funny anecdotes in the histories of both parties.

When Lida and Mrs. Cristi found each other in the bathroom, it had the flavour of a clerk trying to sell his employer. The conversation was an important one for late morning, though they were talking of Lida's Everett. Mrs. Cristi was beginning to have her doubts of that affair. They had sprung up, these doubts, not long after Lida's preoccupation had lessened the number of evenings she could spend on double dates with Mrs. Cristi. The girl, she told herself, was a little fool. She gave warning:

"You're getting so you think of nobody else."

"Well, why should I think of everyone else? He is plenty good enough for me."

"Yes, he's a dentist, and he acts like a gentleman, not like some of these fellows one meets in this country. At the same time, Lida, a girl makes a mistake when she ties herself up, and holds herself too cheap that way. Putting all her eggs in one basket."

"What way? He loves me—and I'm crazy about him. Ain't that alright?"

"Yes. It's perfectly alright, in some cases."

"Why ain't it all right with us?" Lida demanded. Her hands were idle, and she made no pretence of washing the stockings she wanted to wear when she went out with Everett that night. "Why ain't it all right?"

Mrs. Cristi made a movement of impatience. "Lida, don't you see? He'll never marry you."

Lida straightened her neck and threw back her head. "Oh, is that what's bothering you! That old gag! Why he's so crazy about me he'd marry me tomorrow, if I'd let him. Whenever he talks about a ring or anything I just change the subject." She laughed. "I guess I know what I'm doing," she added a little belligerently.

"Nonsense! Lida, you're just a child. Sometimes I wish—I wish, well, I hadn't encouraged you to—to go about with men. They're no good. Not one of them's worth—"

"Not my Ev. You don't know my Ev. Mrs. Cristi, unless you're really in love you can't know what a man's like. Why, he'd do anything in the world for me—"

"He won't marry you," said Mrs. Cristi sharply.

"What?" said Lida, startled. "Aw, you don't know what you're talking about. What, what makes you think—that? Did somebody—tell you something?"

"I know he won't. He'll never marry you. I know just the way his mind will work. He'll think, now I'm a professional man, and I'm making good money. Pretty soon I'm going to be well off. Well,

I'll wait a few years, and then I can marry anybody I choose. That's the way they look at it. Don't you worry, I know all about men."

She was interrupted by a loud thumping in the pipes. She hastily turned the tap and let out a stream of steaming water. The panes of the little frosted window began to weep.

"You don't know Everett," said Lida sullenly, taking up her stockings, and preparing to leave the room.

Mrs. Cristi was bent forward to the fast-clouding mirror, looking herself carefully in the eyes.

"When's your next engagement with him?" she asked.

"He's taking me out tonight."

"That's one thing: you go out with him too often. If you want him to marry you, you should keep him guessing. It's not like my man, Bernic. His wife told him to get out, and he's very glad of any little crumbs of kindness." She was giving Lida an answer. The girl said tartly:

"Never mind, I'll get someone for you tomorrow night, somebody with a car, that'll take us all to the Palais Royale."

"But my dear! What has that to do with it? I didn't mean—" She gave way to her annoyance. "Well, you're just a little fool. You'll see how it'll turn out."

Lida had turned the catch of the door, but did not open it. She sobbed. "My God, Mrs. Cristi, what am I to do? I can't help it, can I?"

"You just watch in the future. Keep your eyes open and see if you don't think I'm right." Mrs. Cristi called down the hall after her maid.

Green Eyed Monster

Miss Campbell had only one regular caller to her room, a young man of about her own age who, like herself, had taught school for a few years in out-of-the-way places, but who was now, as he said, in business in Toronto. Usually he met her downstairs to go out, but occasionally they spent the evening in her room. She had a guitar, which he strummed by the hour, and they could feel the two students in the next room listening. Sometimes Edmund would come up, peek into the open door, and Miss Campbell in her sweet, used-to-children voice would call him in. Donald would give Edmund candy or gum, though he never could be urged to take more than one piece, and hold him on his knee.

Sometimes they turned out the light and told ghost stories. Edmund would grow very still and scared; he preferred animal stories. Edmund thought that Donald was a very wonderful man, dark and stoically calm like his father. And Donald had not even pretended to take him for a girl. If Miss Campbell was going out with him, Edmund at least had the pleasure of going up to her room to announce him.

If they stayed in, Donald usually went home at about half-past eleven; and when one night he stayed till then minutes to twelve, Miss Campbell apologized to Mrs. Cristi. Parting at the door they had met Lida and Mrs. Cristi and two men coming in. One they supposed was Everett took off his hat very politely.

"My dear, it's perfectly alright. Let him stay till two o'clock if you like. It doesn't make any difference to me."

"Oh, but Mrs. Cristi!" exclaimed the girl, taken aback. "That would be too late, in my room."

"It's alright. We know you're a good girl, and he's a good boy. As for people who speak evil, if they'd just look at home…"

So after that they did not pay much attention to the clock, but talked and laughed and played the guitar and made fudge and love to their hearts' content. Miss Campbell told Donald with great amusement of her conversation with Mrs. Cristi, and ended, "As though I would let anyone else come up to my room." Sometimes they omitted to leave the door open. One night this circumstance, with the aid of Edmund, precipitated a lovers' catastrophe.

Edmund came to the door, which was opened a crack, and seeing a man sitting on the trunk inside, he pushed it open.

"Hell—o!" said Donald.

"Oh!" said Edmund, breathless. "I thought it was Mr. Bedlington."

Miss Campbell could have wrung his neck, but she smiled sweetly, and said:

"Edmund, you said you were going to get me a key for my room door, do you remember? So that I could lock my room when I went home for the Christmas holidays."

Edmund now took his finger from his mouth. He had been looking at Miss Campbell with round-eyed awe, knowing that something was wrong.

"Oh, yes, Miss—I'll get it right now."

The girl began talking rapidly and Donald was willing to let her run on for a few minutes before he questioned her about the Mr. Bedlington the boy had expected to find in her room. Then Edmund came back, with a key.

"Miss Campbell, here it is. This key fits your door, and it don't fit none of the other doors."

"That'll be fine, Edmund," said Miss Campbell sweetly. They tried the key in the lock and it worked. Nothing much was being said and, finding something unsympathetic in Donald's attitude that night, Edmund ran off. Then began a conventional lovers' quarrel. Donald demanded the history of this Mr. Bedlington. Miss Campbell told him that if he looked at it that way, she'd never tell him. If he wanted to be such a big suspicious—then he could. She wouldn't tell him a thing about it, for it didn't amount to anything anyway. That was alright, Donald admitted, but no matter how innocent, it looked strange to have a man in one's room, and a man he had never heard of, a man she didn't even want to tell him about, after saying she wouldn't think of letting anyone else in her room.

Well, there it was—if he didn't want to believe her that it was alright, she would tell him nothing. They parted for the night rather early. Going out with him in the hall and down a flight, Miss Campbell continued her righteous quarrel, in whispers, not two yards from Mr. Bedlington himself, who was visiting old Mrs. Webster again with his concoction for colds.

Edmund ran out at them from the shadows, exclaiming gleefully.

"I bet you don't know what I got! I got a key that will open *all* the doors!" He showed a skeleton key, and carefully inserting it into Mrs. Webster's door, clicked the lock back and forth.

"See, it fits 'em all."

"Edmund, you mustn't do that! You'll scare the people that way."

"Come on up to your room and I'll show you how it'll open your door."

Donald, in no mood for friendly badinage with the boy, looked down at him with a grim smile, and continued to the first floor.

"Goodnight, Donald," called Miss Campbell gaily over the

banister not accompanying him farther.

"You won't tell me, then?"

"I don't mind your thinking the worst, because the worst is not very bad."

"Yes, you told me so. Well, goodnight."

Christmas Negotiations

It was only four days until Christmas. Miss Campbell had gone to her small-town home, the law students were about the house all day, and Mrs. Webster was even more stiffly polite than ever. Bill got a temporary job driving a department store delivery wagon, and made a joke about automobiles going to the bad and horses coming back into style. Only four days before Christmas, and the Cristis did not know where they were going to spend it.

The children began talking about it openly, and before the day was out even Mrs. Cristi realized that time was passing, and that something would have to be done.

When Edmund saw that discussion was permissible, he wailed:

"I wanta go to Daddy's. There won't be no Christmas here."

Baby snarled at him. "Shut up. Mamma won't let you go. There's not going to be any Christmas." She hoped that her mother would hear this.

Mrs. Cristi spoke to Belle out in the kitchen.

"I'd better have Baby 'phone him, don't you think? We can't let it go on over Christmas."

"Well, for my part, it can go on as long as it likes. I don't care if I never see him again," said Belle, with an air of restraint.

"Oh, we'll call him up and see…" Mrs. Cristi did not seem to have her accustomed certainty in dealing with this matter. She went to the drawing room, where Baby and Edmund were playing.

"Mamma," said Baby, "can't I call Daddy up?"

"Oh, for Heaven's sake, yes! Call him up, and get it over with. I suppose you want to bring him here for Christmas."

A smile overspread Baby's ironical features, and she moved toward the 'phone in the hall. She sat down on the little chair in front of the instrument carefully, gave the order for the long distance operator, then the number very politely and surely, and waited. Her mother stood beside her, at the stairs, and Edmund came running in. Belle was banging things in the kitchen.

"Hello, Daddy."

"Hello, that's you, Baby, is it?"

"Yes, Daddy. I'm coming out to see you, Christmas."

"That's fine. You're all coming, aren't you? Mother's bringing you all out here, isn't she?"

"I don't know, Daddy. I'll ask her. Belle doesn't want to come, of course, but I'm coming for sure. And maybe Edmund. Just a minute, Daddy, and I'll ask Mamma."

"Let me have the 'phone," said Mrs. Cristi, stepping forward.

"No!—wait!" Baby's ever-ready temper rose. "What's that, Daddy? Alright, I'll talk to Mother."

Baby reluctantly handed over the receiver and rose.

"Hello, Lucas!" called Mrs. Cristi. His name had once been Luigi. "Hello-hello!"

"How are you these days, Emmeline?"

"Oh, there you are! What do you want to talk to me about?"

"Why, Baby said you wanted to talk to me. She's thinking of bringing you all out here to see me."

"Oh, is she indeed? Perhaps the rest of us might have something to do with that."

"You mean you have made other plans for the holidays?" asked Mr. Cristi's careful voice.

"I don't mean anything. We might come. It depends on how we're welcomed. If you want to make a joke out of it—"

Belle came running into the hall, and adjured her mother sternly.

"Don't give in there now. Don't give in. Don't you give in."

"Why, Christmas time, we should all forgive each other and be happy," adjured her husband's voice reasonably. His reasonableness had always maddened her.

"I don't know whether I can get away or not. I don't think I can myself. I have a large house here to attend to."

"Ask the children," said Mr. Cristi.

"It's no good asking the children!" snapped Mrs. Cristi.

"It is! It is so! I'm coming, Daddy!" screamed Baby. Belle almost laid hands on her, but didn't dare.

"Belle won't come, I know that. And I think Edmund will want to stay with his mother—"

Suddenly Mr. Cristi lost his temper. A yell came over the wire.

"She won't come, eh? You tell to Belle she comes out to visit me *before* Christmas, or you needn't any of you come. She's never been out to see me yet. You can call it all off if Belle won't come out and see me."

"Oh! Such a man! Such a temper! I *won't* quarrel with him. I *won't*!" She put the receiver down on the table and rose. Baby took it up.

"Daddy, what's Mamma mad about? I'm coming anyway. She can't stop me."

"Oh, well, you can come and bring Edmund. But you can't all come unless Belle comes out to see me once first. She never has yet."

"Oh, Daddy," wailed Baby, breaking under his grim tones, and her mother's screeching. "Don't get mad and talk that way. She'll come sometime, she'll come soon and see you." He did not answer, and she looked about for someone to take the receiver. Her mother and Belle had gone into the drawing room, and before they could appear, Edmund took it up.

"Hello, Daddy. Daddy, this is Edmund speaking."

"Yes, I know, Edmund. How are you?"

"I'm alright, Daddy, but I don't like it here. I want to come home."

"You can't come home unless somebody brings you, and I don't want you all to come unless Belle comes out to see me first. She never would come."

"Aw, Daddy!" Edmund began to cry. "Don't be mad at us! Belle'll come. I want to see you so bad!"

"Alright, Edmund. Don't cry. I'll see *you*, anyway. Be a good boy, and I'll have something nice here for you, Christmas Day. Tell Mother to come to the telephone, will you?"

"Can I, Daddy? Will you? Oh, Daddy, that's great! That's swell! Just a minute and I'll call Mamma. Mamma!"

Mrs. Cristi came running swiftly from the drawing room. This time Belle did not follow her. "What, what is it?"

"Talk to Daddy."

"Hello—hello!—"

"Well, is Belle coming out to see me? If she does, you can all come for Christmas, and stay as long as you like."

"They wouldn't care to stay long in that barn of a house."

"I'll try to make it as comfortable as possible. What do you say?"

"Well—she doesn't want to. I'll try and get her to go, but the child of her—I mean, the child has a mind of her own. I don't pretend to rule her!"

"Child of her mother, you meant. You say she'll come this afternoon?"

"If she comes at all, I dare say she'll come this afternoon."

Christmas Holidays

Lida was left with the whole house to look after. She did not mind the job. She knew what looking after it got usually, and she was not burdened by the prospect of equalling that. She would sweep the stairs and halls occasionally, because the roomers would notice any difference there. Of course, there was the water overheating in the morning and the coalman bringing truckloads of coal. She paid little attention to him, but it was strange how he knew she wasn't the daughter of the house. Bill was with the Cristis on the farm, but Mr. Bedlington could look after the furnace just as well—though he was meddlesome. He even looked as though he would like to tell her about not wearing stockings in the house. Just let him try! It wasn't him that was running the risk of catching cold, just to save her good stockings so she could wear them when she went out with Everett.

No, Lida was going to have a good time once. No kids to bother about or get in the way, nobody using the 'phone when she wanted to use it—the Cristis used the 'phone more than all of the roomers combined. Only her own meals to get, whenever she felt like getting them. Mr. Bedlington got his own breakfast, and didn't come back till night. He pretended to keep an eye on her, but she scarcely ever saw him.

Goodness knew she needed some sort of a chance like this.

Everett was not the same anymore for some reason. For a while, he had taken her out or come to the house or she had gone to his office every night. Then he had slackened. It wasn't because she tried to keep him away to make him keener. She had thought of Mrs. Cristi's advice, but she knew it wouldn't work for them. She was crazy about him and she had thought—she was sure he had proven to her – that he was crazy about her. Now it was different. Funny how things could change in the twinkling of an eye, and you didn't even know they were different. But they were.

Now was her chance. She'd fix things definitely this time. Maybe he'd ask her to marry him. Oh, how could you make things definite, when promises and oaths didn't mean a thing unless you—both of you—loved each other? And love was such a quicksilvery thing... At various periods during the affair with Everett, and even before, she might have thought she knew what it was to be in love. But she was learning all the time. Terrible. And if things went wrong, there could be no outlet to the mix-up.

Lida alternated between the kitchen and the hall. In the kitchen on the table she was cutting out a piece of green crêpe de chine, which Mrs. Cristi had given her as a Christmas present for a dress for herself. Mrs. Cristi didn't expect her to try to make it herself, but she had to, for Everett. She worked with feverish haste, for fear she might not get it done, for fear he might call first. But what if he did not call at all? He *had* to call, for she could not wait to see him a single night. The dress would be so becoming. It *must* be worn tonight. If he doesn't come—she stitched still more feverishly. Before night she saw that she couldn't really undertake finishing it. She had cut it out and basted the pieces together. She could picture it, picture how it would look when they swept across a ballroom floor. But her dashes to the hall were unavailing. He didn't call, and the telephone never rang for her.

She called him up. That fool of his, Zimmie, answered. He would forward her message, he said. The doctor would call her.

She hung about the hall all day, ready to spring upon the 'phone, wildly tripping downstairs to find that the call came from one of the Cristi creditors. She said rapidly, "Go to Hell, they're away for Christmas." She almost swore at them over the 'phone. But Everett didn't call.

Meanwhile, she had some fun with Bud Maxwell, the kid about her own age who was trying to go with her. It saved her life. She used to give him a date now and again. When he called her on the 'phone, she lavished endearing names upon him in a sweetish falsetto. He never failed to fall for it, and thought she was a swell kid. She drove him nuts. "Well, goodbye, sweetie darling," she would tell him at the end of half an hour's talk and, hanging up the receiver, she would nod her head and giggle: "Didn't I kid him along, though!"

Then her smiles left her as she thought of Everett. He might have been trying to call when she was talking, and the operator would have told him, "Line busy, sir."

At last he did call up. There were only two days left before the Cristis would return. She had spent Christmas in the house alone, not even going out to a restaurant for Christmas dinner, for fear he might come for her at the last instant. She explained to him that she had charge of the house now, and waited for him to ask, "When can I see you?" After some talking, he did.

"Are you busy this afternoon?" she asked him. "After office hours, I mean?"

"Why—what? What do you want to see me about?" His tone was suspicious and somehow alarmed.

"Oh, nothing," she answered jauntily. "Only old Mr. Bedlington comes in at night, and he's so suspicious if you have anyone in your room."

"I see. Well, I wouldn't have to go to your room. We could go out someplace tonight. Would you like to dance?" She knew his poker voice. He thought he was doping something out.

"No, dear," she said, almost shyly. "We could go out if you wanted to. I just thought you might want to have supper here with me, cooked all by my little self. Then if my cooking didn't kill you—"

"Ha! Ha! You're alright, Lida. All right. I'll come over shortly."

He came over, and he stayed to supper, but he left right after, before Mr. Bedlington got home. The dress, which she had put on in the shape it was, fell flat. He only stared at it and she did not have the heart to ask him whether he liked it. It was sleeveless and seemed out of place in the kitchen. But then, somehow she had pictured herself sitting on the chesterfield. The second afternoon he came again and she did not wear it. He went away as early as the last time, but he left a little present—a couple of suits of silk underwear.

No Anchor But Anger

A few days after, Miss Campbell came back to resume her teaching, her sister arrived, another dark girl, taller and heavier, healthy-looking. She was resuming work in an office, and she intended to stay with the Cristis only a week or so until she had found an apartment. Her husband was an advertising solicitor and at times a freelance journalist. He was coming on in a day or two. They had been in Montreal for some time, but had decided to come back to Toronto.

Mrs. Cristi welcomed Mrs. Helyar with great effusiveness. She told her what a lovely girl her sister, Miss Campbell, was and how they had known at once that they were kindred spirits, and had been like sisters to one another. Anyone connected with Miss Campbell was welcome to her house and any room in it. They were delighted to have her and her husband. When was he coming? Today or tomorrow? That was splendid.

The next morning, the two girls went out together and Miss Campbell came back late in the afternoon. Her sister did not appear until about seven-thirty, and she brought her husband, a ruddy-faced, stocky-slender fellow with a way of looking at you as though he might want to laugh. He had met his wife after work, she had told him of the arrangement with her sister's landlady, and they had dinner in a restaurant.

Mrs. Cristi greeted them briefly, and it seemed that her interest in this young man, strangely enough, was lessened rather then increased by his connection with her friends. He was favourably impressed by her monosyllabic stage-English manner, her way of wearing her hat and earring, and by the old house itself.

"You see," he explained to her, "we are going to look for an apartment, so we will not want a room for more than a week. I expect it will be that long, though, because our things haven't arrived yet from Montreal, and I have some business before I can get around to moving."

"Well, that will be *just* alright. Oh, we've lots of rooms. No trouble at all. If you want to go sooner than that, or stay longer, even make your headquarters with us permanently, in fact, we'd love to have you." She was speaking, of course, to his wife.

Miss Campbell, Mrs. Cristi, and Mrs. Helyar stood exchanging amenities for a moment, while the young man regarded them with a half-smile. Belle came in and took Mrs. Helyar's arm familiarly, her face glowing with good-nature.

"Now, Belle's ready to show you to your room," said Mrs. Cristi. "I know you don't want a large one for just a few nights."

Belle led the way to the back room on the second floor in which the doctor-dietician had lived. It was small, but well heated, and it would do. The couple stood talking, while Belle at once rushed away to get clean towels and clean linen. Then Mrs. Cristi appeared in the hall.

"Come here! This way! I want to show you another room, quite large and light, with a fireplace—" she opened the door into the front room in which Miss Campbell had first made her acquaintance and that of Bill and Edmund. "But there's no light in it because Bill broke the fixture. However, it would be fine in the daytime, with a good desk, you see, and you can have it," she addressed Mr. Helyar, "to do your work in."

They agreed that this was fine, and so the matter was settled. The next night they met after work as before, looked at a number of apartments, ate together, and reached the Cristi place at about half-past nine. Going to their room, they found it lighted and the door partly opened. Their luggage was not inside, but a man's overcoat on a hanger, and a pair of trousers hanging by the suspenders, were in the closet. Their combs and brushes were still on the dresser.

Astonished, they looked at each other. "Let's go up to Emma's room," suggested the young wife. "She may know something about it."

Helyar laughed. "The mystery of the vanished clothes. Are you sure we're in the right room?" He thought he knew enough about people to know their things had not been stolen.

In the hall, a lean-visaged, unshaven man coming out of the bathroom met them. He went into their old room. The young wife's brow was wrinkled with troubled puzzlement, amazement, as she stared after him.

"The thot plickens," grinned the young man. "Come on. We'll find they're given us a better one."

In Miss Campbell's room they found her and Donald, strumming the guitar.

"Oh, kids," said Miss Campbell. "Did you get your apartment alright? They've rented your room here."

"Well, they're going to give us another, aren't they?" asked Helyar.

"Why, I don't' know. No, I guess not. Mrs. Cristi thought you'd be getting an apartment and she had a chance to rent it permanently, so she did."

"But good gracious!" exclaimed Helyar, warming up. "What right had she to assume that we were going to move away today when we were renting the room for a week?"

"I don't know," shrugged Miss Campbell. "She spoke to me about it, and I said yes, I thought you'd be getting an apartment soon, I didn't know she was renting it right away." Her brother-in-law looked at her stupefied.

"But Emma," said her sister in a gentle complaining voice. "It's so unreasonable. Where are we to go tonight?"

"Got no place to stay the night, eh?" Donald grinned.

"I guess we can find one," growled Helyar. "Find out what the old girl means."

"Dear, you'd better call up that apartment we liked, and say we'll take it right away. They might let us in tonight."

"Yes, we'd better, if we're going to have all this sort of mix-up. But they wouldn't let us in tonight. What would we sleep on?"

"They have those wall beds, and we could borrow blankets from Emma."

Time was going, and after further discussion it was seen to be ten-thirty. Mr. Helyar thought he would 'phone, but Mrs. Cristi was using the telephone, had been for fifteen minutes, and apparently would for fifteen more.

"Well, pack up your things, and we'll go to a hotel tonight, and we'll get an apartment tomorrow, for sure." He went downstairs to their room and searched for their belongings, bringing away the brushes. The new occupant said nothing.

At length they descended the stairs, Mr. Helyar bearing two suitcases and his wife a club bag. He had decided to have no words with this sort of woman. He set down the suitcases and taking off his hat and settling his shoulders in his overcoat, waited for Mrs. Cristi to terminate her 'phone conversation.

She was preoccupied and did not notice the two. She tapped her foot indignantly as she talked, and her hat and even her earring nodded to give emphasis to her words. "Yes—I do mean it—come over here—Oh, right away—at once. Or I'll never—yes, at once," she gasped. She banged down the receiver and brought her long straight back to an upright position.

"Type of an unreasonable woman," Mr. Helyar reflected. "I pity her husband, if she has one." Aloud, he said, "Mrs. Cristi, I hear that you have rented our room, so we are going away. Here is the money." He extended two one-dollar bills.

"But it's three dollars!" exclaimed Mrs. Cristi, not heeding his first remark.

"No, it's not," he returned with decision. "It's really only one dollar, and I'm giving you two. You told me we could have the room for a week for seven dollars, and we had it one night. That's one dollar."

"Oh, but I charge a dollar and a half per person when I rent it for one night. That's three dollars."

"You didn't rent it for one night," he reminded her. "You rented it by the week, and I'm paying by the week."

"Oh, Max, give her the money," said his wife, plucking his sleeve. "Let's get away."

"No, I'm not doing anything about your renting the room over our heads, but I'm not going to pay you extra for doing it."

"I don't understand you! You're the most unreasonable man I ever saw!" exclaimed Mrs. Cristi. "I don't understand it. You said you were getting an apartment—"

"Within a week or so, I said."

"Oh, Max, come on. Give her the money she asks."

"I really shouldn't give her any, but I'm paying her double." He extended the bills again. Mrs. Cristi shook her head, baring her teeth. They could hear men's chuckles in the drawing room. This seemed to increase Helyar's determination.

"I won't take it. I'd rather take nothing. You couldn't get a room in a hotel for that."

"I wish I had. They wouldn't have rented it away from me, and I'd have known I had to get an apartment."

"But you don't understand. Miss Campbell! Miss Campbell!" screeched Mrs. Cristi. "You're the most unreasonable people."

"What is it Mrs. Cristi?" came high, sweet tones from the third.

"Come down here. Come down at once."

Miss Campbell came down to the last turning and leaned over the banister.

"Now don't scream at me like that, Mrs. Cristi, or I won't answer you. Now what's this fuss?" Mrs. Campbell replied.

"Miss Campbell, didn't you tell me these people were hunting an apartment?"

"Yes I did, Mrs. Cristi."

"There!" Mrs. Cristi turned to the Helyars. The young wife was in an agony over this controversy. Her sister was quite cool about it. But the other two seemed to have decided that nothing would reconcile their claims. "I told you, didn't I? Now give me my money, and go. You try to insinuate I'm tying to take advantage, and it's you who are—"

"What – difference – does it make – what Miss Campbell told you?" Mr. Helyar pounded one fist on the other palm, endeavouring to stem the other's flow of words, his voice filled the house. "You – rented – us – that – room – for a week. I'm paying you by the week."

In the midst of this uproar, Mr. Bedlington appeared from the kitchen wearing his hat. He skirted the fighting group in the hall. "Excuse me!" he begged softly, though no one heard him, and went into the drawing room to hold a whispered conference. "Excuse me!" he said again, coming back, and went outside. Young Helyar understood that he had gone for the police, and knowing his own rights, hoped that it was so. But magistrates always believe women…

Mrs. Cristi quieted swiftly. "Take it, oh, I wouldn't take it as a gift. I'd rather not have anything for keeping you if that's the way you look at it."

But Mr. Helyar put the two dollars into her extended hand, and departed without another word.

Miss Campbell slowly wended her way upstairs to Donald and

the guitar. On the second landing she met a doleful looking Lida, who grinned at the sight of her.

"She found her match for once."

Lida's Father

One morning, when the affairs of the house appeared to be in an unusually serene state, an eruption occurred of certain significance and of dire terrorizing circumstance.

It had been a nice morning. Mrs. Cristi had got up and got her own breakfast; she finished it by ten o'clock. Belle and Lida had both taken baths, which had somewhat allayed the overheating of the water and the general morning steaming-up of the house. Baby had gone to seminary on time. Edmund and Bill were out of the way and playing in the basement. Mrs. Cristi recalled the piece of green crêpe de chine she had given Lida for Christmas, and decided to make it up into a frock that morning. She asked Lida about it, and found that the girl had cut the dress out by patterns in a woman's magazine, and basted it together. Mrs. Cristi was pleased. There was nothing to do but go ahead with the making of it.

So there they were, the three of them in the drawing-room, at the big bow window; Lida, her hair nicely brushed, freshly bathed, and with no stocking, was in the sleeveless new green dress, which was pinned to her in some miraculous way which did not allow it to fall. Mrs. Cristi, pins in her mouth, walked around her with satisfaction, "taking it up" here, and "letting it out" there. Belle was holding a broom in one hand and a magazine on her knee, while she sat on the davenport. Occasionally she would look up and comment favourably.

Suddenly there was a jangling repeated ring of the doorbell.

"You go, Belle, we're busy," said Mrs. Cristi.

"Is Lida O'Ryan here this mornin'?" asked a thick but piercing voice.

Lida was covered with confusion. "It's my old man. What's he want?"

"Keep still, or you'll spoil it," advised Mrs. Cristi. "I'll see him."

He had swung aside the curtains and stood under the arc, a thick-set, blond, red-faced man with flashing blue eyes. Lida herself was dark, and quite different from him. She just stood looking at him.

"Well me girl!" he roared in an out-of-doors voice. "And here ye are, getting dolled up for more devilment." He paused ominously, drew a long breath, held it as though for an outburst, then slowly released it. "You get into some Christian clothes, and come with me. Git! Upstairs with ye."

"That's no way to talk to your daughter, sir!" interposed Mrs. Cristi quickly. "You might try to be a gentleman for her sake."

"An' I'll have a few words with you while she's gone, Missis," Mr. O'Ryan added, lowering his head and looking at her as though she were some animal he was stalking. "I'll just tell ye what you are, first. You are a bawdy-house Missis, an' there 'y'are, take it or leave it."

"A what? Sir! You come here to insult me?" Mrs. Cristi advanced to him, hands clenched.

His voice sprang at her in a roar, his face became red, his hands stirred hugely.

"A whore-house-keeper!" he bellowed. "I said it. And it's the courts that ought to look after you. Don't say a word, or I'll take you and your whole grist of tarts to court. Ruinin' good girls that have decent parents. Do you know what you need?"

Mrs. Cristi had been speaking, but he deafened her. Now at the rhetorical question she made herself heard. She stretched forth an arm. Her words came with lightning-like swiftness.

"Go. I won't have you in my house even to wait for your daughter. You disgrace her. I shall protect her against you."

"Go, is it?" he demanded more quietly, almost grinning. "She's going, and I've a good mind to take you along and leave you at the police station for the keeper of a common bawdy house, ye slut! Do you know what ye need? A good horsewhipping's what ye need, and pity 'tis ye've no husband to give it ye. A pity," he added, wagging his head regretfully.

Mrs. Cristi grasped at a straw.

"You've been drinking. You'd better go now. You'll be sorry for this. If you go now, I'll say nothing about it."

"Sure, you're condescending!" sneered the man. "Maybe it's in Paris ye think ye are; where your kind of house is licensed. Anyway that makes no difference, ye're ruinin' decent girls. Ruinin' them! And ye should be took directly before a magistrate. He'd straighten ye up, my lady! He'd give ye a dressin' down. He'd *send* ye down, for a year or so, where ye could cool off and come out a decent woman."

Mrs. Cristi, her ears red, silent, almost beside herself, sped toward the door, but he barred it. She dashed to the other side of the curtains and tried to break through, but his arm shot forth and she was wrapped in the curtain and his arms. There was a heavy muffled thud as his palm took her, as she judged, in the right place, and after a scuffle she released herself, scarlet, trembling. Lida was standing there, dressed for the street.

"Sir! Sir!" Mrs. Cristi cried. "You are impossible. I'll have you arrested. I shall. For assault."

The Irishman grinned at her, almost as gleefully as fiercely.

"Don't let your courage get the best of yur judgement. When the man that did my girl wrong goes to jail I'm sure the jail would

113

be only too pleased to accommodate your ladyship at the same time. Come on, Lida."

They left the house with a bang. Mrs. Cristi threw herself on the davenport and wept for half an hour. Belle had slipped to the kitchen when she had answered the doorbell. She came in and tried to comfort her mother, who cried as she never had before. Both spoke as though they did not know what the man had meant. But the dentist, if he took Lida there, would tell him that he had always seen her in this house. They broke down anew.

And what the roomers would think! Mrs. Wells, right on the ground floor, surely she was in. And Mrs. Webster, just one flight up. They would have heard most of it. But then Mrs. Cristi took comfort. They would have heard her scream, and threaten to have the man arrested. They would know who was in the right. By and by they calmed down, but Mrs. Cristi could not forget that she had had such words addressed to her, and she hadn't been able to get revenge as she could on her husband. Oh! Life without him was even more impossible than it had been with him. "If I could only die," she moaned.

In the afternoon Lida and her father (a very changed and silent Lida with him) came back. "I want me girl's things," declared Mr. O'Ryan. "And I want them all. Lida, girl, search this house till ye get what's yours."

Mrs. Cristi and Belle walked to the kitchen at their best pace, leaving him in the hall. Later, Belle went upstairs to help Lida pack.

"I'm sorry, Lida dear. What happened?"

Lida's tears began to fall and she sank on the edge of the bed before the open suitcase.

"Oh, I'm sick! He doesn't love me one bit. He told father so before we left. Oh, oh!" She moaned into her handkerchief.

Belle put her arms around her. "Did you go to see Everett?"

"Father took me there, to his dentist office, where I'd never been before—hardly—and oh—what—" she sobbed. "Who do you think was there?"

"He was, I suppose. Any patients?"

"He was there, *and his wife.*"

"And his wife!" gasped Belle. "I didn't know he had a wife."

"Neither did I," moaned Lida piteously. "*He* never told me... His wife was there and he was there, and Pa made such a ruckus. I just feel as though everything was dead inside me."

Belle did not answer.

"And he called me and him such awful names."

"What did Everett say?"

"I—he said he didn't mean any harm, he thought he was—was being good to me, taking me out to places, and then—then—"

"Oh never mind, dear. It seems bad now but wait a while and it'll blow over. He was no good anyhow. Lida, you're well rid of him. Married—my God! That's men."

"I could stand it all if it wasn't for him." She began to dry her eyes. "And now I've got to go back and live with my stepmother, and she won't ride me! I always hated her," she added listlessly, looking at the half-filled suitcase. "Belle, did you have my brush and mirror?"

Climax For Creditors

Belle was accustomed to taking her baths in the morning, in order to lessen as far as possible the force of the explosive thumpings in the pipes due to overheating from the furnace, and the consequent necessity of letting the water run in the bathroom, to the effect of a most steamy and opaque atmosphere throughout the house. This showed a most unusual forethought and enterprise on her part, because the water was hot enough at any time of the day to take a boiling bath. But taking it in the morning helped out, so Belle did, as soon as most of the people were away.

So it came about that the morning after Lida's departure, Belle was taking a bath in the middle of the morning, while her mother, naturally, was sick in bed for the day. Baby had gone to school, and Bill was out seeing about some job. Edmund came screeching to the bathroom door:

"Belle! Belle!"

"What's the matter, can't you wait till I get my bath? What is it?"

"Oh, Belle, there's two men downstairs, they want to see Mamma and I told them Mamma's sick," said Edmund in his polite voice, so that Belle had to stop her splashing to hear him.

"Well. Did they go away?"

"No, they're waiting to see you."

"Tell them I won't come."

"I told them you were in the bath, and they said they would wait."

"Oh, Lord!" said Belle with a furious groan.

When she came downstairs she found the two men ensconced in the drawing room as though they meant to stay. They were the grocery man, McCready, and the furniture man from whom Mrs. Cristi had bought those little knick-knacks which make such a difference in a place, and give it an air. Belle didn't know what to do with them. She listened meekly to first one and then the other, as he pressed his claim, and related how he had given credit and waited and given more time. At first she thought that they were employed by the same firm, until she got it straight that they had just chanced to be inspired to visit her at the same time and had been let into the house together. They co-operated admirably, however, waiting patiently for one another's claims, and taking turns in threatening lawsuits and seizures. Belle told them at length that the bric-a-brac man could take his furniture, if he thought he'd rather have it than money; and as for the grocer, he could not seize anything else, because they owned nothing else in the house.

"Who's your landlord?" he demanded.

Belle did not reply.

Finally, they went away, promising that her mother would hear from their solicitors. Greatly relieved at staving them off with nothing, Belle went upstairs and told her mother about it. Mrs. Cristi was not relieved at all. She had been trying to listen, and the mere absence of the men meant nothing to her since she had not fully realized the terror of their presence. She sobbed into her pillows, and conveyed to Belle that the whole world was leagued against them, as it always was against the widows and the penniless. What would they do?

"Well, there's always Mr. Bedlington," said Belle in her candid way.

"Sometimes I think we've got nearly all we can get from Mr. Bedlington," said Mrs. Cristi. "You know he didn't like it when you bought that fur coat, though he didn't say anything, and he pays the twenty dollars a month. Why the other day—" But she stopped. She would tell Belle that Mr. Bedlington had actually asked her when she was going to pay him some rent. It would place the girl at a disadvantage. You had to have some confidence.

"Oh, shucks," said Belle. "I can get anything I want from Mr. Bedlington. All I have to do is sit on his knee. And he thinks I'm such a nice girl. He tells me to go to Sunday School. Gosh, Ma, he's dumb. But he's a suspicious old fool. He's been sneaking around on the third floor trying to watch me and Bill."

"It's very nice of him, dear, to give you such good advice."

That night Mr. Bedlington seemed in such a solemn mood that they did not know how to approach the subject. He had his supper with them, and then began working at his carpentry in the basement. After a time he called Mrs. Cristi down there. They had quite an earnest conversation, and a long one, and finally Mr. Bedlington was made to see that there was nothing he could do but pay the furniture man and the grocer part of what was outstanding for the present, and perhaps soon Mrs. Cristi would be able to pay the rest. But she would have to be careful, and not spend any more than she could help.

"Well, I won't buy a thing. I can't buy a thing. My conscience wouldn't let me, now that I see how matters stand," she declared.

Mr. Bedlington did not reply to this, but he told her how these people had hunted him up where he was working. Mrs. Cristi was angry. The idea of their bothering him about such petty things! He said dryly that it was all right. There was a formal note to their parting for the night.

As if all this were not enough, Mr. Bernic called, and instead of being nice to her in the way he used to be, he seemed ready to quarrel, and even hinted that he remembered lending her money.

She wept and told him that in view of the circumstances she thought he might overlook it. But he was willing to be frank, and they parted stormily, at an early hour, not later than eleven-thirty.

So Dark! Or The Hindu From The Window

Mrs. Cristi was in a pensive mood. She sat in the window of her drawing room more of the time than she did anything else, moodily watching the life of the quiet street. She knew everyone living in the houses and apartments by their goings-out and comings-in. She was starting to try to cultivate friendships with some of her neighbours. Edmund liked the boy next door, so she let him go there to play, or had the boy over to play in her house. There was a difference to the boys in the two arrangements. In the Begrie house they had to be quiet. At the Cristis' they could litter the halls with toys so that no-one could approach the 'phone, slide on the carpet, slide down the banisters, shout, and shoot off their toy guns. At the Begrie's there was a maid in uniform; at the Cristis' Belle made a batch of cookies for them. The quiet little Begrie boy became just like Edmund in that house. Baby and Marian Begrie, thirteen, spent afternoons together embroidering. Baby was embroidering a factory cotton stamped apron for her mother.

In the same house next door lived a Hindu gentleman. Mrs. Cristi watched his goings-out and comings-in with a great yearning. He was above medium height, very very swarthy, with glossy black hair, and he was stout, almost fat in the face, with a look of wise good-nature, as of one who would not willingly disturb his digestion. Mrs. Cristi enquired of him from Mrs. Begrie but could learn nothing beyond the fact that he taught in the University and had a little roadster. It was enough to allow her to form a complete portrait. She would look after him rapturously as he walked along, exclaiming:

"So dark! He's *so* dark!"

Mrs. Webster came hobbling with difficulty into the drawing room, and doggedly traversed the length of it to sit down opposite her landlady at the bay window.

"Mrs. Webster, don't you think it's true that a person should marry a man of the opposite complexion? I'm very fair myself, you know." She added this because she was not wearing her hat, and her hair seen at a distance looked almost grey. So her mirror had reiterated of recent weeks.

"There is some old saying to that effect, isn't there," assented Mrs. Webster in sociable vein. "Your husband is very dark, isn't he, Mrs. Cristi?"

"Oh him! He's an It—an Englishman, and that's Norman blood. He's not really dark, like an Easterner, a Hindu for example. Have you seen the Hindu gentleman who lives with Mrs. Begrie? He's so dark. Don't you think it would be *wonderful* to be married to a Hindu?"

Mrs. Webster, eying her throughout this speech, said non-committally:

"I can't say that I have ever considered such a thing as being within the bounds of probability."

"Oh, yes, I suppose at your age you look at it that way. But people do marry Indians and Hindus. Don't you remember reading in the newspaper about that Canadian girl who married the Maharajah?"

"No," said Mrs. Webster firmly. "I never read about it. My eyes and my health in general have been so poor that I have restricted my reading to my Bible of late. No, I can't say that I've ever heard of such a thing."

"Oh!" Mrs. Cristi thought that Mrs. Webster might be a little more *comme il faut*, a little more a woman of the world who could make allowances for other people's points of view. But you had to make the best of people, and she did so herself. "How have you been lately, Mrs. Webster? It must be two days since I saw you."

"I've been fairly well, considering. Belle hasn't brought me the clean pillow cases and towels I told her to get me the other day."

"Oh, we'll see about that right away, Mrs...." interjected Mrs. Cristi, absently staring out of the window.

"But I wish I could get out more," went on Mrs. Webster calmly, her large jaws working with each word, and her eyes turned up as though above the rims of spectacles. "Though I'm usually glad of the fact that I don't have to get my own groceries. If I couldn't 'phone up and have them delivered, I would have to go out, and perhaps that would do me good."

"Oh, no, no, Mrs. Webster. At your age! Think of it! And in the winter! I should say not. Why I never think of going out for groceries myself, and I'm far abler than you, though of course my health is so undependable."

"No, I suppose I should be glad of the advantages I have... It's my back that bothers me the most, aside from being a cripple."

"Oh, my back is terrible, too," exclaimed Mrs. Cristi. "Why are we women made such martyrs to our healths? And my neck. It's neuritis that I suffer from most of the time. Some days I feel as though I couldn't lift my arm. You know?" She looked at Mrs. Webster enquiringly, but Mrs. Webster maintained a steady regard.

"Well, it's terrible to be a cripple," she sighed at last. "So far from people helping you and having a regard for you, you have to struggle to get your own."

"Oh, heavens!" exclaimed Mrs. Cristi, staring out of the window. A wagon was turning into the drive beside the house. "There's the coalman with another load of coal. I wonder whether Belle's got things fixed up down cellar. As soon as the bin gets empty the boards are carried away."

She sank back into her chair and began talking again.

"It is change that people need. Various contacts. There are so many interesting people in the world, of various nationalities, and one owes it to oneself, does one not, to meet them and learn about them? You must meet my neighbour, Mrs. Begrie. She is the lady whose little boy comes over sometimes to play with my Edmund. And that Hindu gentleman stays with her... I think the evening would be the best time to call."

"I wouldn't go out in the evening," said Mrs. Webster. "I'm not taking such chances as that with my health."

Vaccinations

There was nothing, Mrs. Cristi decided, like nipping things in the bud, taking stitches in time, and that sort of thing. It saved you so much trouble later. When she decided to clean the house, she cleaned it, every inch, and diverted none of her attention to anything else. And it stayed cleaned, till the thought occurred to her again. The same with anything else. She had been reading in the papers about the small-pox epidemic. There had been several cases in Montreal, and several suspected cases already in Toronto, the enterprising newspaper stated. Mrs. Cristi made up her mind. She would have no such affair for her children. Bedrooms shut up, doctors and nurses coming, the kitchen turned to making special sick dishes, oh, she knew what a heavy sickness meant. You couldn't get out when you wanted an evening's recreation. And besides, think of the expense.

No, she would have none of that. The children were going to be vaccinated, and she would have no more worry about it for the rest of their lives. She told Edmund and Baby they need not go to school tomorrow, and she went to make an appointment with a doctor. The doctor seemed to prefer the day after that, so she arranged with him that he should come to the house and vaccinate all three children.

Arrived home, she explained that the doctor was going to make them well for the rest of their lives. Edmund said he'd run away to school, but when his mother told them that a mistake had been made, and they were to stay at home the following day instead of tomorrow, they set up such a howl to stay home tomorrow too, that she finally let them.

When the doctor did come, all other activities in the house were suspended. He brought his serum, a quantity of cotton batting, and those little short quills with which he scraped the skin from the arms of the children. Belle was done first, and she was so bold about it that Edmund stopped crying to watch. Then came Baby, who set her teeth and said never a word. And Edmund, though his lip trembled, did not cry after it was done. The doctor, of course, was very jolly about it, and overlooked their looking on it as a sort of ordeal, almost a calamity. When he was done and putting away his things into his little black satchel, he asked: "Now aren't you glad you're never going to get small-pox?" And they had to admit that they should be glad. Edmund became quite interested in watching him. Mrs. Cristi was very dignified, so that he did not even mention that the bill could be settled later.

When Miss Campbell got home that afternoon, Mrs. Cristi marooned her in the bathroom and told her proudly what had been done. She found that Miss Campbell was taken quite as violently as herself with another idea. The girl bit her lip, and told her how her little sister had been vaccinated and all that had happened, and she told Mrs. Cristi what vaccine was made of: the puss from wounds of horses and cows infected with the disease. Her descriptions were vigorous and full of loathing and putrid terms. Mrs. Cristi, fascinated by the picture Miss Campbell's words called up, finally screamed in horror:

"That awful doctor! Why didn't I tell you about it before? That *villainous* doctor! He never told me a word about that and I'll never pay his bill—or at least I will see that he knows my opinion of him."

In a few days something seemed to be troubling Edmund's eye. It was red and swollen, and finally he confessed that he might have been scratching his vaccination scar, because it was awfully itchy. The eye got worse, until it almost closed, and he could scarcely see out of it. It looked terrible, and his mother sighed and wondered if she shouldn't get the doctor again. Miss Campbell said by no means. She got boric acid, and had Belle bathe the eye in hot water solution. She felt sorry for the poor little kid, going about so patiently with his sore eye. But when he came up to her room to listen to Donald's stories, she didn't cuddle him on her lap. She felt a dull repugnance for the very object of vaccination.

Reviewing the vaccination spasm, she saw it as another of those impulses of her landlady's, which seemed to strike without warning or discrimination. She took a sarcastic satisfaction in reflecting that it as lucky Mrs. Cristi hadn't become obsessed with the idea of decapitating the children instead. In fact, Miss Campbell began to wonder whether it were the people, the house, or herself, becoming stale.

Points Of Vantage

Since Donald's misunderstanding with Miss Campbell regarding in the identity of Mr. Bedlington, he had not been over to see her more than two or three times. They appeared to forget that coolness, and then something would bring up the subject and the eternal quarrel would begin again. One night in February he called her up by telephone and suggested that he come over to see her that night. She forbade him very earnestly; she was tired. That was not a good enough excuse for him, so she confessed explicitly that she had been reading some letters to the editor in the evening paper, about women's rights, and that she was going to write a letter to the editor herself in reply, which would put the whole matter in a new light. She needed the whole evening because she might have to rewrite it and she wanted it to be in the paper right away. Donald finally submitted, and told her he would be watching the paper for her article.

Miss Campbell thereupon took out a glass jar of ginger sticks, a pad of typewriting paper, pen, and ink, and after divesting herself of most of her clothes and putting on slippers and a heavy bathrobe; she sat down at the table, took the pen in one hand, a large stick of ginger in the other, and set to work.

There was a knock on her door, and she called come in, thinking it might be Edmund or Belle. Mr. Bedlington entered and sat beside the door on her trunk. He was very sad and needed cheering up.

The Cristis, he confessed, had driven him nearly to the end of his rope. They wouldn't pay their rent, he told her frankly now; and these other relaxations of theirs, fur, coats, grocery, furniture, coal bills, and the like, were a substantial embellishment to their primary obligation. He didn't know what to do with them. They never seemed to have a cent.

"They seem to think," he concluded, "that all they have to do is to come to me and they can get what money they need."

"Oh, Mr. Bedlington, they don't really? That's too bad," commented Miss Campbell.

"But I still think that Belle's a good girl. You know I'd do a good deal for her. And she's so good to me. She would take good advice, if it wasn't for her mother."

"Perhaps you're right," agreed the girl. "By the way, Mr. Bedlington, I have to go down and see Mrs. Webster a minute, do you mind? I'll take her down a piece of the Christmas cake my mother made for me since I'm going. Then I've got to finish my article. I'm sorry."

They went out of the room together and parted downstairs. Mrs. Webster was sitting in her armchair, reading the *Last Days of Pompeii*, which Mrs. Wells had lent her.

"My dear," she said. "I'm very sorry indeed. I know I should like your mother's Christmas cake, if I were permitted to eat it. But the doctor's orders are that I am to abstain from cake. Have you ever read this book? It gives a wonderful picture of ancient times. I can very easily believe that if they were to dig down where they least suspect them. Why, my dear, right here in Toronto I know of one such case which came under my personal observation. It was when the Erinbragh Apartments were being built, and I lived in the house next to it. My oldest daughter and son were only five or six years old then—forty—forty-four—no, forty-three years ago, that's it. They found the hull of an old boat away down under the earth when they were building the foundations. But I'm ahead of my story. It wasn't actually under the Erinbragh. The circumstances were like this: When they were digging the foundation for the building, they found the ground was all hard clay so hard that they had to cut it out in slabs and blocks. Well, then after the building was put up, the same contractor began building another apartment house over a couple of blocks. This time when they dug the foundation they found the subsoil was sand, soft sand, and it wouldn't hold the building up. So the contractor suddenly had a bright idea. He began digging blocks of hard clay from the vacant lot behind the new apartment house, the Erinbragh—yes, funny to think it was once—oh, very up-to-date, very tony as they used to say, most respectable. Well, from my back veranda next door, you see, I could see them excavating this clay. And by and by if they didn't come across the front end of a boat. It must have been five or six feet down. It was lying across the boundary of the lot, so they cut through it just about in the middle. I've often thought afterward that I should have gone to the Historical Society and got them to put that boat in the Museum. You see it was a very large boat and might have been used for rowing or sailing. Yes. Or both. It wasn't an Indian boat, everybody agreed to that. It was made of oak, immensely thick, not the least bit decayed. Clay had preserved it. It must have belonged to the first white men that came here—the French. Why did they drag it so far inland? That's just what I'm coming to. It's about three miles from the lake shore now, as you know. Well, I've often thought about it since, and the way I have reasoned it out is just this. The shore line has been added to a little every year, hasn't it? Even in your time it has stretched out a long way from the Union Depot to where the Docks are." The girl shook her head stubbornly. She didn't know. She didn't quite want to flee from this interesting and untimely information. "Then think what it would do in four hundred years."

They began talking about the Cristis, the major topic of

conversation in that house. Mrs. Webster shook her head gravely. She didn't know just what to think about it all, she declared.

"You know, I am living right on the same floor as her bedroom. She may think I don't hear the hours she comes to bed and all about it, and when her men go out. She may think I don't know a thing, but I've heard them. She forgets there's a transom over my door." The girl looked up. The transom was a quarter open. Mrs. Webster hastily continued. "If you ask me," Mrs. Webster concluded, her big face staring up into Miss Campbell's and blinking rapidly above her imaginary glasses, "I don't think the woman's straight. I know how to sum a woman up. The goings-on I hear! I haven't lived seventy years for nothing. I don't see how she can be straight. You don't know what you'd hear if you were on the second floor here with me. I'm glad you're not, and can't see it all. Child, I'm glad you miss it all. It's only the warmth of the house that keeps me from moving to a decent place."

"Well, Mrs. Webster," whispered Miss Campbell. "I could tell you something. You don't know the things I *see* on the third floor."

Mrs. Webster goggled, and gaped, then shut her mouth, and went on talking. "But what gravels me most, is the way the woman pretends she's sick. It's just sheer pretence. The only reason she can't get up in the daytime is that she's been up all night."

After an hour of agony, Miss Campbell got away to her room. She had jumped out of the frying-pan into the fire, but after cursing a little she began her letter to the paper and kept at it steadily until she had it rewritten and ready to mail. After reading it over with satisfaction for the last time and putting it into an envelope, she saw that her watch reported three o'clock. She would wash and retire immediately.

Before she opened the door she thought she heard a movement, and stooped to look through the keyhole out into the hall. There was no transom above her door, and she could hear nothing. Nor could people outside know whether she was still up, while she stood in that position.

Belle and Bill were coming out of the vacant room next to the bathroom. Belle's large form looked very fetching in pink silk pyjamas, which Mr. Bedlington must have bought. She had her arms around Bill, pulling him toward the staircase. He was unwilling to go, and she kissed him a great deal en route. Miss Campbell could hear him whisper.

"Why can't you stay a little longer, Belle? Your mother's not gone to bed yet, you don't want to disturb her."

"Yes she is, I've got to go."

"Naw, her fella isn't gone yet."

But after a few minutes of very thorough embraces they parted and Bill went to his room in the back. Miss Campbell sighed.

"Well, I wish Mrs. Webster could have seen this." She shrugged her shoulders, recalling how Belle had long ago tried to deceive her by assuring her of things which Miss Campbell would have taken for granted in a girl of her age and farm upbringing.

England, My England

Sometimes days would pass without the various persons in the house seeing anything of each other, beyond, perhaps, passing the time of day on the stairs or in the vestibule getting their ice-topped milk bottles. Then chance would throw two or three together and they would talk an afternoon or evening away. For several days after the closing in of the creditors, the Cristis were satisfied to leave things to chance. But one day Mrs. Cristi knocked at the bathroom door when she knew Miss Campbell was inside, and unbosomed herself of her current attitude to the world

"I'm so sick of this house, Miss Campbell! So sick of it! I can hardly bear to pass a single hour in it."

"Oh, I'm sorry Mrs. Cristi, haven't you been well?"

"Oh, you know, Miss Campbell, we're not used to this sort of life." She sighed. "Nobody could make this house pay its own way. Oh well! Doesn't matter! I don't care. Not now. Perhaps I'll be glad it was so bad. I'm going to England now."

"To England!" exclaimed the girl. "But isn't that splendid. When did you decide to go?"

"Oh, I've been thinking of it for a long time. Belle's going to stay here of course, Mr. Bedlington wouldn't agree—agree to let us give up our lease altogether you know. But Edmund and Baby and

I are going to England."

"How soon are you—"

"How? Oh, first class, of course. I have to be comfortable when I travel. Oh, how soon? In a month, I expect."

"So soon! It must cost a lot, doesn't it?" Miss Campbell thoughtfully dug her little finger into her ear, and reflected that it was time she was cleaning her toe-nails. "The toe-jam—oh, I mean, the tourist traffic must be heavy in the early summer, is it not?"

"Yes," snorted Mrs. Cristi, straightening up from the wash-bowl. She was wearing a brassiere so low that it was nip and tuck. "But that's the time when you can wash the most—oh, I mean enjoy it the most, so we may as well go then. By the way, Miss Campbell, wouldn't you like to go along?"

The girl gasped. "Go along with you to Europe—why I—oh, Mrs. Cristi."

"To England." Mrs. Cristi smiled. "We'd like to have your company and one more wouldn't cost much when there's a party. You needn't worry about that. If you want to go, that is. I can arrange it, alright."

"Oh!" Miss Campbell had begun to think. This sudden affluence could only mean that Mr. Bedlington had got so sick of them that he was bound to be rid of them even at the cost of sending them to England. "My job, I'm afraid, would be gone when I came back."

"As you please, my dear," said Mrs. Cristi, draping her towel on her forearm with stately mien, and stepping out of the bathroom like straight-flanked Diana. "We'd love to have you, all the same. I tell you—you think it over."

"A—alright, Mrs. Cristi, I'll think it over."

But that night, for some reason, Mr. Bedlington came up and sat on Miss Campbell's trunk and made a clean breast of things. He had become so desperate to get rid of them, and they had kept at him so hard, that he had practically made up his mind to pack them off to England if they would leave him alone. He would run the house himself. Belle might stay or not, it didn't make much difference, but he'd just as lief she stayed, so that she would be away from her mother's influence. And she might be of some help in the house with him. The responsibility would do her good.

Miss Campbell almost lost her temper. He would regret doing that, she told him. When they got to England, they would have no money. They would be sure to keep sending cables, unprepaid if possible, asking for more money. He would have to bring them back to Canada. They would never rest until they had got him to pay their way back.

"Maybe I'd be getting into worse trouble than I'm in now," suggested Mr. Bedlington meekly.

Miss Campbell did not want to meddle in the affair at all, she told herself, but she could not quite stand anyone being made so big a fool of, whether she liked the other party or not.

"You certainly would," she assented. "You don't know how much you'd be getting into. Besides they have a father, and he might call you to account I don't want to queer their game, but if you want to look about for yourself, Mr. Bedlington, the best thing you can do is to get them out of your house, and trust luck to get your rent later. The best thing for them, too. You're really wronging them, little as you intend to. Giving them a wrong attitude toward life. Soon they'll think they don't have to work for what they get."

"They do have it kind of easy, don't they," said Mr. Bedlington. It occurred to him that even women had to work if they could get no man to support them. He might have been regarded as an easy mark in the affair, he saw. "But it can't go on." He set his jaw. "There's only one thing I want: to get rid of them. I'm at the end of my rope."

He looked at her admiringly. "You know, if I only had somebody level-headed like you to help me look after things… By the way, you spoke of Mr. Cristi. He came to see me today."

"He did, he did! What is he like?"

"Why he seems to be in the same position with them as—well, as I am. He says he disclaims responsibility, since they have left him of their own accord. He has posted a notice in the paper: not responsible for any debts contracted."

"Is that a scheme to beat you, too?"

"No, no. He did this as soon as she left, I guess."

"But what's he like? Mrs. Cristi has spoken of him so often—"

"He's a good fellow. Says if I can't stand the expense any longer, the only thing to do is evict them. I suppose he would just as leave I did; they might come home then."

Miss Campbell shook her head impatiently. She knew Mr. Bedlington wouldn't understand if she asked what the man looked like, and he couldn't describe him in any case.

Mr. Cristi Comes Into His Own

A year later, when spring had at last predominated over winter in a struggle beginning in January, at the end of April, Miss Campbell received a postcard written in the hasty, angular hand of Mrs. Cristi. She knew at once who the sender was, in spite of the puzzling signature. Would she come out to the farm to visit them Saturday? Mr. Cristi would be away and they could have a long talk, and the children of course would be delighted to see her once more. So the following afternoon, Miss Campbell climbed aboard an interurban car.

It stopped in less than an hour at a little box of a waiting room which stood on a side-road, and down the road the small wiry Miss walked to the second farm. She saw a large, weather-beaten grey barn that had been raised upon a high cement foundation wall recently, a windmill, little outbuildings which might have been chicken and pig pens and ice house, and finally, hidden in a group of cedar and spruce evergreens, a small white-painted house.

As she crossed the little wooden bridge, to the lawn, Edmund came running with a dog, gave her one glance and a sedate, "How do you do, Miss Campbell," and ran around to the back of the house. At once the front door opened and Belle came out and threw her arms around her. Mrs. Cristi, in reply to screams, shouted down that Miss

Campbell was to come up to her bedroom, but before Belle and Miss Campbell had exhausted the first spate of questions, she appeared, attired in the dignity of a bathrobe, and received her visitor as if they had parted only yesterday, with her old flattering easy familiarity.

"Oh, my dear, I've been hoping against hope, that you'd come out and see us here. I wouldn't ask you in the winter, for we have no hot water and no bathroom here. Oh, the winters!" She looked about the room sadly.

"Oh, but I think your place is lovely—and in the summer it must be simply heavenly!" Miss Campbell hastened to exclaim.

"Oh, I might have managed the heating and plumbing, but I didn't want to leave it all here. I am hoping against hope that Mr. Cristi will sell out and go to England, where one can live like a social being."

"And you have your rooms furnished so lovely. That's a darling radio, and those curtains…"

"Oh, I'm thinking of getting a phonograph and a new rug. I miss the phonograph we had in town. You remember. In the house where you were, I mean."

"How did you like it where you were after you left Mr. Bedlington?"

"Oh, very well. Of course we did not have a house, we just had an apartment, and of course there was no income. I didn't want to spend all I had saved keeping roomers, so we came back, when my husband came and begged us so hard. Belle wanted to stay, of course."

"Oh, I liked it alright," said Belle with a toss of the head. "Some people talked about Mr. Bloxham, but I thought he was a nice old man. He always treated me like a daughter, anyway. I never saw anything out of the way. He was nice to me, a gentleman. Gee, he used to take me to shows."

"Well, people will gossip so," interposed her mother. "You know those two girls who went just before you came. When they heard we'd bought our furniture from Mr. Bloxham and he used to come over, they said he had a terrible name. I think they wanted me to understand that was why they were moving. But there was nothing in it. When we went to live there, he was a perfect gentleman, took Belle and me to shows and for car rides, and treated each of us nice."

"That's fine," said Miss Campbell cheerily. "And how's Edmund?"

"Pretty well, thank you, Miss Campbell," said the boy, manoeuvring the buckle on the collar of his dog, which he was holding. "How's Donald—I mean Mr. Houlahan?"

Miss Campbell blushed. Belle grabbed her left hand and admired the diamond on the third finger. Something quiet, like awe, came into her round vivacious face. "Where's Bill?" Miss Campbell asked in turn.

"He's in Detroit. Calls me on long distance. Wants me to come there. I got mad the other night and hung up on him. But he's a dear! Maybe I will go. Only Mother'd be so lonesome here in this dump without me." She indicated the surrounding farmhouses and general countryside, not the house itself or its furnishings. "Mr. Bedlington didn't use to like Bill. Gosh, that man used to make me laugh."

Miss Campbell gazed at her noncommittally.

Mrs. Cristi seemed to feel called upon to answer a query. "Miss Campbell, I haven't the slightest interest in the man." Still Miss Campbell said nothing. "Are you still teaching those children in Rosedale?"

"Yes. I live there now."

"Are you going to keep it up?"

"No." She blushed again.

"Oh, what are you going to do?" Belle exclaimed.

"Well, my plans are rather indefinite."

"Marry Mr. Houlahan?"

"Oh, but you've got them mixed. It's Mr. Bedlington's ring."

For once they were all silent upon this new Darien.

"Mr. Cristi and Baby have gone fishing," remarked Mrs. Cristi, "this afternoon. He promised her to go some Saturday afternoon, but it hasn't been nice these last few weekends. Belle, put on some tea for Miss Campbell. And bring those cakes."

They admired one another's clothes, and talked comprehensively for a couple of hours. Then Miss Campbell was about to walk to the car, when Baby and her father came in.

"How do you do, Miss Campbell." He shook hands with her gravely. Baby has been telling me about you. How kind you were to her and Edmund."

Miss Campbell looked up at the tall man who was as dark as herself, though his eyes were grey-blue and accustomed to long ranges. She was puzzled at his accent.

"I hope I don't seem surprised," she said. "When Mrs. Cristi told me you were an Englishman and liked being out of doors, I pictured you as the conventional blonde type."

"Oh, I'm not English particularly as my wife is," he answered. The girl hardly heard him for Mrs. Cristi was speaking at the same time.

"Miss Campbell was just going," she said. "She doesn't want to miss her car, or she'll have an hour's wait."

"I was just telling Mrs. Cristi how much I like her home. It's lovely out here."

"These things," said Mr. Cristi, waving at the radio set, "are not my buying. The farm does not pay so well, these times. But *she* buys them. I tell her to keep her money, save it."

Mrs. Cristi bridled.

"Well, when I went to the city I made good. I could make good again for that matter. Come outside my dear and I'll show you the cutest thing."

"You know," she added, when they were outside, "I never have time nor strength for a flower garden, and neither has Belle—time, with the house to look after. But look here what Baby's done. Virginia Creeper. Isn't it nice."

"*Isn't* it, though! Such a nice idea."

A little stake in the ground held one end of a string, and a spike driven into a window-sill the other. Up the string climbed a tiny vine in tendrils which would grow to thick root-like vines and long leaves.

"It will look just like ivy," said Mrs. Cristi.

"Well, goodbye, Mrs. Cristi."

"Goodbye."

The End

Raymond Knister

May-June, 1928, Toronto
December, 1930 Port Dover

Raymond Knister, born in Ruscom, Ontario, is recognized as one of Canada's first modernist writers and is considered a pioneer in the development of Canadian Literature; working amongst prolific Canadian writers such as Frederick Phillip Grove and Morley Callaghan. Knister began writing short stories early in his career before moving to Iowa City to write and work as an associate editor of *The Midland*. During this time he became interested in the modernist movement and published his early stories in the Parisian journal, *This Quarter*, alongside James Joyce, Ezra Pound, Ernest Hemingway, and e.e. cummings. Later, he published many of his stories, sketches, and poems in other periodicals such as *The Midland, Voices,* and *The Canadian Forum*. He published two novels, *White Narcissus* in 1929 and *My Star Predominant* was published posthumously in 1934. *There was a Mr Cristi* is yet another excellent example of how Knister explores a unique manipulation of reality and the human psyche in playing with immoral characters in unusually circumstance.